Denny, From
another, NEH,

Laurie Anderson

MISERY BAY

Misery Bay

And Other Stories from Michigan's Upper Peninsula

LAURI ANDERSON

NORTH STAR PRESS OF ST. CLOUD, INC.

Library of Congress Cataloging-in-Publication Data

Anderson, Lauri.
    Misery Bay : and other stories from Michigan's Upper Peninsula / Lauri
Anderson.—1st ed.
        p. cm.
    ISBN 0-87839-178-9 (alk. paper)
        1. Michigan—Social life and customs—Fiction. 2. Upper Peninsula
(Mich.)—Fiction. I. Title.

PS3551.N37444 M57 2002
813'.54– –dc21   2002069232

Cover photo by Lauri Anderson

Copyright © 2002 Lauri Anderson

ISBN: 0-87839-178-9

First Edition: June 2002

Printed in the United States of America
by Versa Press, Inc., East Peoria, Illinois

Published by
North Star Press of St. Cloud, Inc.
P.O. Box 451
St. Cloud, Minnesota 56320

Dedicated to
The people of the Copper Country

Misery Bay is both real and fictional. The real Misery Bay is an unincorporated township on the south shore of Lake Superior in the Copper Country of Michigan's wild and wonderful Upper Peninsula. It's an extremely isolated and profoundly beautiful place populated mostly by people of Finnish descent. How it got such a name, I can't imagine.

The fictional Misery Bay is made up of stories in this book. All of the stories are fiction. Any resemblance of characters to real, living or dead people is purely bad luck.

Coppertown

Chapter One

Toivo and Eino

For years Toivo had been receiving offers of millions of dollars from various magazine sellers. All of the offers guaranteed that Toivo had won the money fair and square simply because he lived at his current address and because, presumably (though the offers never directly said so), he was a nice guy. The only hitch was that Toivo had to mail back the acceptance form within a month and then a bushel of hundred-dollar bills would be sent to him in short order. The magazine sellers always indicated that it would be nice if Toivo subscribed to a couple of their magazines, too, if he were so inclined.

Toivo had never taken them up on their offer. He didn't think they'd mind. After all, if they had so much money that they were willing to give him a couple of million for no apparent reason, why would they care if he declined to subscribe to a ten-dollar magazine? Plus, the long letter that informed him that he'd won millions invariably stated that he didn't have to buy any magazines unless he felt like it, and he rarely felt like reading any-thing, especially in English. Of course, Toivo subscribed to a couple of Finnish-language newspapers out of Duluth, Minnesota, and Superior, Wisconsin, but those were socialist papers and were not among the maga-zines sellers' lists. And, so, for years, Toivo had mailed back the offers of millions on the very day he'd received each offer in the mail, but, lately, he'd grown weary of the task because no money had yet arrived on his porch floor, where the mailman dumped his mail every day around two o'clock in the afternoon.

So, when the latest offer arrived in his mail, Toivo picked it up, put it in his shirt pocket and went next door to have coffee with his old friend Eino. Eino was in his back yard raking the last of the fall leaves into the alley that ran behind his workshop. For late November, the weather remained very warm—in the low forties—creating the kind of day that Toivo and Eino liked to enjoy by puttering around outside. After all, soon the heavy snows of December and January would arrive, and then they'd be buried under three hundred inches of the white stuff until April. Winter was an especially cruel season in Michigan's Copper Country on the south shore of Lake Superior.

"I've got a problem," Toivo told Eino.

The two went inside to drink coffee and eat *nisu* and seek a solution. They sat around the yellow Formica table that Eino's deceased wife, Hilda, had bought at Sears in 1952. In 2000, the table, nearly indestructible, still sat in the middle of the kitchen, its metal legs and its rock-hard surface as solid as ever. "This table will outlast both of us," said Eino as he sat down and tried to rub the ache out of his eighty-eight-year-old left knee.

Toivo told Eino about the money he had not yet received. "Did you write to them?" Eino asked.

"Once in English and twice in Finnish," explained Toivo.

"Did they ever answer?" asked Eino.

"Heck, no," said Toivo. "Not unless you count the form letters that I get from them every couple of months."

"Let me see one," said Eino.

Toivo showed him the latest letter from one of the companies. "This isn't a form letter," said Eino. "It's addressed to you. It mentions your name several times. Plus, it's really friendly. These must be nice people."

"They may be nice, but there's something wrong with them, too," replied Toivo. "I asked them a couple of times in perfectly good Finnish to give me an exact date when the money would arrive, and they ignored the question. If they're so excited about giving me 2.4 million dollars, then why don't they just do it? Why do I have to fill out more and more of those damned contest forms when I've already won?"

"Maybe you have to take the bull by the tail and look him right in the eye," said Eino. "Or maybe there's another kind of problem here—something you haven't thought of."

"Like what?" asked Toivo.

"Maybe it has something to do with political correctness," said Eino.

"What are you talking about?" asked Toivo.

"My granddaughter was over for a visit yesterday," said Eino. "She teaches something called feminist studies at the Finnish college in Hancock. She had a lady friend with her, and I listened to their conversation while they had coffee and *rieska*. I learned all sorts of stuff about today's young people. They're pretty crazy. They're all politically correct. Political correctness means you have to be very careful about what you say or do, especially if you're a WASP."

"That doesn't make any sense," said Toivo. "A wasp is an insect. Sort of like a bee."

"This is a different kind of wasp," said Eino. "WASP is an abbreviation for someone like you or me. It stands for white Anglo-Saxon Protestant."

"Explain that," said Toivo.

"You're white if you're from Europe," explained Eino. "It doesn't really matter which part of Europe either. You could be English or French or Croatian or a Finn. All of us are just lumped together and then discriminated against."

Toivo remembered his youth in the Copper Country when the mining towns all had a very obvious pecking order. The real Americans with British names like Smith or Jones were on top. They owned the mines, most of the land, and even the houses where people like Toivo's parents lived. For a long time, the Finns were at the bottom of the pecking order, and times were hard, especially when people like Toivo's parents tried to organize the miners. The bosses with the British names had brought in Pinkerton thugs to beat up pro-union folks, and on Christmas Eve in 1913, they'd murdered seventy-two children at a party in Calumet. Some of those dead had been neighbors, and most of them had been Finns.

"How are we discriminated against?" asked Toivo.

"The government now has lots of rules that give preference to women and minorities when it comes to going to school or getting a job," said Eino, who had worked in the mines for more than forty years, which was probably why he had bad knees, a bad elbow, poor sight, frequent backaches, and an odd catch in his right side.

Toivo was stunned. "I have a great-grandson who's a senior at Hancock High School. He wants to go to Suomi College next year. He's one-hundred percent Finnish, and his name is Paavo."

"He might not get in," Eino said sadly. "Women and minorities now get first choice."

"But he's a Finn," said Toivo.

"That might work against him because all Finnish men are now considered Anglo-Saxon," said Eino.

"What's that mean?" asked Toivo.

"It means they consider all of us to be British," said Eino. "And rich and privileged," he added.

"So, it took until I'm eighty-nine, but I'm finally equal to the English in this country," said Toivo, pleased with the idea.

"That's right," explained Eino. "But by these rules, which are called Affirmative Action, you're both equally at the bottom of the pecking order."

"Are Swedes and Russians also Anglo-Saxon?" Toivo asked.

"I suppose so," replied Eino. "They're both from Europe and get lumped in with the rest of us."

Toivo didn't much like the idea of being lumped together with Finland's traditional rivals. "Well, my great-grandson still should be okay," he said. "He goes to Church every week, and Suomi is a Lutheran college."

"That might work against him, too," explained Eino. "Lutherans are Protestants. 'Protestant' is the 'P' in WASP. Plus, Lutheran is the wrong kind of Protestant. A lot of minorities are Baptists. Jesse Jackson, for example. Maybe you should send the boy to a Baptist church.

Toivo scoffed at the idea. "So, what you're trying to tell me is that I might never get my money because I'm one of these WASP people," said Toivo.

"That's right," said Eino. "Maybe they're holding onto the money to see if you convert—to see if you become a minority or a woman or something."

"That's crazy," said Toivo.

"Equally crazy things have already happened," said Eino. "My granddaughter told me that Jews and Japanese are WASPS, too, because they both make too much money and do too well in school."

"So, Japanese are English?" asked Toivo.

"I guess so," said Eino.

"How about Chinese?" asked Toivo.

"They're probably English, too," said Eino, "because their kids are really good students, and they make a lot of money in this country."

"And how do women fit into all of this?" asked Toivo.

"Women are the majority so they're considered minority," said Eino. Toivo shook his head in disbelief.

"I don't understand it, either," said Eino, "but my great-granddaughter wants to be a lawyer, and I wish her luck. She's a cute little thing."

"I guess I'll never get my money, but at eighty-nine, what would I spend it on anyway? Maybe we should take advantage of this last good weather and go fishing," Toivo suggested.

Toivo and Eino went fishing on Portage Lake at least once a week throughout the fishing season. Portage Lake was only a few blocks from their homes. It separated the towns of Hancock and Houghton, which faced each other on opposite ends of a lift bridge. Neither Toivo nor Eino owned a boat, so they rented any one of the many aluminum outboards available at the marina just east of the bridge. Early in the summer, they'd located a deep spot out toward Oskar and had caught perch and walleyes as fast as they could boat them. Since then, they'd never been able to find that same spot.

"Maybe we'll locate the fishing hole today," Eino said. "In case we do, I'm going to take this with me." He stuck a magic marker in the pocket of his flannel shirt. "I'm taking no chances. It's indelible," he said.

He got his jacket of the hook in the hall and went out to the car. All of his fishing gear already lay in the trunk. Toivo went home, got his stuff, and they drove to the marina in Eino's twenty-five-year-old Lincoln Towncar. Eino loved the old car, but lately it had been acting up. The day before, he had driven it to the mall, and it had stalled in the parking lot. Then it wouldn't start. Fortunately, some forty-five-year-old youngster had helped him out. The fellow knew a lot about cars and had the Lincoln running within half an hour. Still, the car was getting old. Eino dreaded getting one of those new cars. "They're so tiny," he told Toivo. "Even the steering wheels are so small that they're for little kids."

There were half a dozen boats for rent at the marina. They picked one, paid the man, threw in their gear and journeyed up the long, narrow lake toward Oskar. The boat's motor was small, and the trip took them over thirty minutes. Then they trolled back and forth, looking for their special spot.

Lo and behold. The last fishing day was their lucky day. They anchored and began to haul in fish. Around five o'clock, when it was already quite dark in the thickening gray winter light, they pulled up anchor. They'd each caught a bucket of fish. Toivo was about to start the little outboard engine for the return to the marina when Eino pulled the magic marker from his pocket, waved it majestically in the air, bent and drew a large X in the middle of the boat.

"What are you doing?" asked Toivo.

"I'm marking the fishing spot," said Eino.

"Eino, you're such a damned fool," said Toivo. "How do you know we'll get the same boat next time?"

They laughed at each other's foolishness.

After he got home, cleaned the fish, bagged them in the freezer and got cleaned up, Toivo decided to call his great-grandson to find out about his application to Suomi College. When the boy came on the line, he was quite excited. "Not only am I going to college there, but I have a scholarship to play basketball," he told Toivo.

After the boy hung up, Toivo felt relieved. *Why did I worry?* he wondered. After all, his great-grandson had been a basketball star for several years at Hancock High School. *A good hockey or basketball player can get in anywhere,* he thought. To heck with political correctness and all those foolish ideas of Eino's.

Toivo felt better than he had before the call to the boy, but he was still resistant to filling out the forms from the magazine seller. *Ah, well,* he thought, shrugging his shoulders, *You can't take a high horse and claim the low road, too.* Toivo filled out the magazine seller's offer of 2.4 million dollars, checked the box that told the company he was interested in the money, checked the other box that indicated that he wanted no subscriptions, put the forms into their fancy envelope, added a stamp and put it in the little pile of bills to be mailed the next day.

Misery Bay

Chapter Two

Heikki

The fall of 1993 turned out to be unusually warm. The day before had been in the low fifties by late afternoon, and the next day threatened the same. Heikki didn't mind. The further he advanced into his eighties, the more that the coming of winter irritated him. On this particular evening near the end of October, Heikki sat in his kitchen drinking cup after cup of coffee. His wife had gone to bed an hour before and so was no longer in the way. But, before she disappeared into their bedroom, she had taken a red pen and drawn a thick circle around the next day's date. Heikki was trying to figure out why she had done that. Close to eleven o'clock, Heikki, too, went off to bed, still wondering about that circle. In bed he couldn't sleep. In his old age, he found that he could easily nod off any time company came around but that late at night, in the comfort of his own bed, he usually found himself wide awake. That was the case that night. He felt restless. His mind refused to slow down. Plus, that red circle on the calendar haunted him.

Then it dawned on him. The next day must be his and the wife's anniversary. He wondered why he hadn't thought of that sooner. Heikki remembered the date of their marriage and began to count toward the present, using his fingers and then his toes, and then his fingers and toes again, and, finally, using his fingers a third time. The next day they would have been married exactly fifty years. People called that the golden anniversary. Heikki wondered why. *You make a mistake that lasts fifty years,* he thought, *there's nothing golden about that.*

By three that morning, Heikki was still wide awake, so he decided to get up and begin his anniversary day early. Plus, there was a hidden benefit to not sleeping. If people came over to congratulate him and his wife later on, he could nod off and let his wife listen to their endless prattle. Heikki's wife was sleeping soundly on the other side of the bed, so Heikki rose silently and carried his clothes out into the hall in order not to disturb her. He carefully shut the bedroom door and then pulled wool socks up to and over the leggings of his long underwear. Then he pulled on his green wool pants and buttoned them. He wrestled a t-shirt over his head and got his arms in the sleeves. Then he pulled it down over the top of his underwear and followed it with two flannel shirts and a wool sweater. Finally, he held everything together with a pair of broad suspenders and slipped on his laceless swampers.

He was ready for the day. He went out to his truck and drove off to explore back roads. On the gun rack in the pickup's back window, he had his .30-06. A box of shells shared the seat beside him. Several sturdy IGA paper bags lay folded on the seat as well. Behind him, in the bed of the pickup, Heikki had his fishing equipment. He also had filled a large thermos with coffee before he left the house, and he enjoyed his first cup cradled between his legs as he drove. In the cool of the cab, the coffee steamed and gave off a rich aroma.

Heikki had two reasons for this trip. He wanted to fill the grocery bags with apples from roadside trees. Copper Country back roads were dotted with abandoned farms whose orchards still produced good apples long after someone had stopped caring for the trees. He would add the apples to the bait pile behind his sauna. Already Heikki had a number of deer feeding off his pile early every morning and late every evening. One was a nice buck with an impressive rack. Heikki wanted to shoot that buck at dawn on opening day of hunting season, only a couple of weeks away, and, as usual, Heikki had modified his sauna into a deer stand after watching an old movie called

The Last of the Mohegans. In the movie, the British soldiers had protected their fort from the French and their savage Indian allies by firing their muskets through tiny holes in the fort's walls. The holes were not much bigger than the gun barrels. In what he considered an act of genius, Heikki had built a similar hole into the back wall of the sauna. The hole could be plugged with a wooden cork wrapped in leather to keep the sauna steam in and give the deer the illusion of being alone at their meals.

The first time Heikki had hunted from his sauna, nothing had gone right. He had carried his rifle into the sauna and propped it in the corner. Then he had undressed and actually taken a sauna while he waited for the deer to begin feeding. Heikki had just ladled water onto the glowing rocks and the rocks had sent that water back up in an impressive cloud of steam throughout the tiny room when Heikki decided to remove the plug and check on the deer. The rush of cold air into the room had instantly transformed the steam into a rain cloud so dense that Heikki could not see his own arm held up in front of him, let alone a deer two hundred feet away. By the time the air cleared, naked Heikki was shivering too badly to aim the rifle at the buck which nonchalantly munched away on apples and moldy cabbage. Then, when Heikki finally fired, he only wounded the buck, which thrashed around on the bait pile while the other deer fled. Heikki ran outside to finish off the animal and was halfway there before he realized that he was buck naked in the middle of an open field at dawn on opening day and that his neighbor, Hilda Maki, was peering with a pair of binoculars out her bedroom window. Heikki had swung the rifle in her direction and had threatened to fire, but she had ignored him until he had waved a certain part of his anatomy. Then she had retreated and closed the blinds, and Heikki, still naked, had gotten to the deer and finished it off.

Heikki had learned from his mistake. He heated the rocks but did not sauna on opening day. He stood in the dry heat until the deer appeared, and each year he had shot a buck in the first five minutes of legal hunting. That wasn't enough for Heikki, however. The real thrill of the hunt came in the illegal hours of darkness. Heikki loved to poach deer. He hated the DNR and loved to thumb his nose at them and their fancy cars and fancy uniforms by taking a deer at night. Heikki had an ideal light for the purpose. It shot an intense but very narrow beam out into a field. Any deer would stop feeding, would lift its head, turn to the light, and stand there, immobile, until Heikki shot it. Then he'd drive home, sip coffee for a couple of hours, and then drive back to pick up his deer. He'd been poaching for over sixty years and had never been caught because he kept his mouth shut. He butchered the animals in his own barn and kept the meat neatly packaged in his own freezer. When his daughter had married, no one had suspected that the beef stew was actually venison.

So, that morning of his anniversary, Heikki drove along, checking out back fields with his powerful light and taking note of which fields had impressive herds. In several of the fields, he gathered apples, put them in the grocery bags and set the filled bags in the truck bed. At some point, the apples would be dumped in the bait pile, but there was no rush.

The one thing about poaching that irritated Heikki was the position of the steering wheel in American pickups. They were always on the left, toward the center of the road. That meant that Heikki had to cross into the other lane to shine a field on his left, and he had to slide across the seat to the passenger window to shine on his right. It was a problem he had never been able to solve.

After several hours of driving back roads, Heikki was ready for some fishing. He drove to the lakeshore just before sunrise. When he arrived, a thick mist obscured the shoreline and water. Heikki dragged his small aluminum boat from the pickup's bed and got it into the water. Then he returned for the small trolling motor that he kept safe and dry in the truck's toolbox. Finally, Heikki gathered together his fishing pole and equipment and threw them all into the boat. Then he launched his boat into the thick mist, into a kind of dreamscape without reality or definition.

On his way out onto the lake, with his eyes useless, Heikki listened carefully to the swishing of the water against the bow, the distant call of an early-feeding loon, the splash of a rising trout. These sounds were set against the magnified drone of his small trolling engine.

Once out from the shore, Heikki dropped anchor. Otherwise, he'd worry incessantly about driving the boat onto hidden rocks or into an unseen shore. He sat in the quietude of the mist, smoked his pipe, drank coffee and waited for the rising sun to clear the air. He baited his line with a night crawler and cast into the surrounding opaqueness. He listened for the soft *splunk* as his hook struck the water's surface. Then he slowly reeled in, waiting expectantly for a sudden tug on the line. Heikki recast several times before he caught a fish. The brown trout came over the side like some kind of apparition and then flopped around in the bottom of the boat until Heikki reached down and snapped its neck.

The pop of the neck joint brought Heikki out of his revery. The fog already began to evaporate as the sun burned it off. Heikki cast his line a few more times with no luck. He was restless again. He cleaned the fish and tossed the offal into the water. He placed the fish in a plastic bag and put it in with the rest of his fishing stuff. Then he started the engine and returned to shore. He reloaded the truck with the engine, boat, pole, and other equipment. He thought he'd have the trout for lunch, but first he'd go to the post office. He'd entered the Publisher's Clearinghouse sweepstakes but had run out of stamps.

Heikki parked outside the post office building and then reached under his seat and pulled out a bullet-proof vest. He'd heard about all those berserk postal employees always shooting their fellow workers, and he wanted to be prepared. A line of little postal trucks hugged the curb along the side of the building. Suddenly, Heikki had a brilliant idea. Those trucks had their steering wheels on the right side so that the drivers could reach out and fill mailboxes. Those trucks would be ideal for poaching deer. Heikki could just lean out the window with his rifle and fire.

Inside the building, Heikki bought his stamps and asked if he could speak to the boss. "Do you want Korpela or Kilpela?" the woman asked.

Heikki said either would do. Mr. Korpela appeared soon from somewhere in the back of the building. Heikki asked the man if he could lease one of the red, white and blue post office trucks Saturday afternoon and keep it until Monday morning. Mr. Korpela said he could not. Heikki explained that the post office workers didn't do anything from Saturday afternoon through to Monday morning. "Those trucks just sit idle alongside the building,"

Heikki said. "I could use one without interfering with your work, and you could make an extra buck."

Mr. Korpela said the idea was absurd. Heikki then wondered if Mr. Korpela knew where he might buy a used postal truck. Heikki really liked the idea of hunting deer at night in a red, white and blue vehicle. It would be like waving a flag. It would make the entire act of poaching patriotic. Mr. Korpela told Heikki to leave.

Heikki felt a bit down in the dumps after Mr. Korpela's refusal. Also, his coffee supply was running low, but he didn't want to go home. His wife would be up and probably planning something for their anniversary. Heikki wanted to avoid her machinations, so he drove to a neighbor's house. The neighbor was a professor of literature at Suomi College. Heikki was beginning to feel that the last fifty years of his life had been a disaster. Maybe his educated friend could make him feel better.

When Heikki arrived, the professor was just sitting down to breakfast, so Heikki joined him for bacon, eggs, pancakes, syrup, and coffee. The professor noticed that Heikki was depressed, so he tried to cheer him up. "You look pretty good for eighty-three," the professor told Heikki. "In fact, you don't look a day over seventy-eight."

That didn't perk up Heikki because he didn't give a damn how he looked and often seemed to go out of his way to look pretty bad. In fact, that day was no exception, with his mismatched green wool pants, his brown suspenders, red flannel shirt, and gray sweater, all of it topped by a yellow wool *tuque* with blue deer chasing each other in a circular design.

While he and the professor ate, Heikki complained about his life. "The wife and I have been married for fifty years as of today," he said.

The professor had his mouth full of food and said nothing.

"These last years she and I have circled around each other like a cat and a dog in a fight. But we don't fight. We don't even talk. It seems like neither of us has anything to say to the other. Maybe that happens when two people have lived together for too long. I drink my coffee and beer, fish, hunt, fart around in the garden, plow snow all winter. I don't even know what she does. Whatever it is, she does it with her women friends."

The professor pointed out that Heikki was a lucky man, that any other woman would have divorced him as a lost cause forty-nine and a half years before if not sooner. The professor said that Heikki ought to buy his wife an anniversary gift just for putting up with him for such a long time.

Heikki said he would consider it but that he was still bored with his life. It was time for him to move on. "It's time to become an educated man," Heikki told the professor. "But not too educated," he added quickly. Heikki didn't want to leave behind his friends Eino and Toivo, neither of whom had gotten beyond the eighth grade. "That's why I came over to see you," Heikki said. He wanted the professor to recommend an author he should read.

"Just one?" the professor asked.

"How many are there?" Heikki asked.

"Thousands," the professor replied. "What kind of author did you have in mind?"

"A storyteller," Heikki said, "and he's got to be good." Heikki explained that being good meant being interesting. "Can you recommend one author who pretty much says what all the rest have said?" asked Heikki. "That way I won't have to read but the one, and I'll already be conversant with you literary types."

The word "conversant" surprised the professor when it came out of Heikki's mouth, but Heikki explained that he'd looked up the answers for the "Word Power" list in the *Reader's Digest* and "conversant" had been first on the list. Heikki had been waiting all week to use the word in a sentence.

The professor thought for a while about potential authors and then offered up Matthew from the *New Testament*.

Heikki immediately rejected the idea. "And don't give me Mark, Luke, or John either," he said. "I had enough of those guys in Sunday School the one time I went!" he said scornfully. "I read Genesis in *Uncle Arthur's Bedtime Stories*. I don't need that either. Are any of these literary authors Finns?" Heikki asked.

The professor had read Melville, Milton, and Maupassant but knew little about Finnish writers, so he offered up Hemingway. "He's a kind of Finn," he said.

17

"That's not a Finn name," said Heikki.

The professor agreed. "Hemingway has no Finnish blood," he said, "but he acts like a Finn."

Heikki wanted the professor to explain.

"Hemingway loved to hunt and fish, and he was prone to flannel shirts," the professor said. "He had *sisu*, too. He could be stubborn as hell sometimes—could even punch a guy out if it came to that."

Heikki thought that Hemingway sounded a lot like himself. Heikki wanted to know about Hemingway as a fisherman. "Did he fish from a boat or the shore?" he asked.

The professor grinned. "He fished both ways."

"Live bait?"

"Yes," said the professor.

"Good," said Heikki. He didn't want to read a book by a dry fly fisherman—the kind that caught trout and then threw them back in the water.

The professor assured Heikki that Hemingway was not a gentleman fly fisherman with an imported split-bamboo Japanese rod.

"Then I'll read him," said Heikki. "How thick is the book?"

The professor gave Heikki a copy of *In Our Time* because it contained Hemingway's Michigan stories. He was about to explain its elaborate structure—the vignettes, the sketches, the chapter linkages.

"I won't read a book that comes with a lecture," Heikki said, eyeing him.

The professor shut up.

When Heikki left the professor's, he sat in the driveway in his pickup and read the first two stories. Then he drove over to Toivo's for more coffee and to show him the book. Toivo pretended to be interested. He opened the book and read the first story because it was only two pages long. Then he read the second because it had only four and one-half pages, big print. Heikki finished his coffee, the twelfth cup of the day, just as Toivo finished the second story. "Neither story makes any sense," said Toivo.

"I don't think they make any sense either," said Heikki, "but I'm not going to tell the professor that."

Heikki left Toivo's and drove down by the lake. He parked the pickup and read one more story because it was about fishing. It was called "Big Two-Hearted River" and was set in Seney. Heikki had been to Seney and, in fact, had fished that very river, only it was called the Fox, not the Big Two-Hearted. Heikki found it hard to believe that a man who was smart enough to write a book was also dumb enough to misname the river. He also felt proud that he possessed this kind of literary knowledge. "The professors haven't got much over me," he said to no one at all, since he was the only one parked within sight.

As Heikki tossed the book onto the truck's floor and turned the ignition, he noticed a blurb on the back of the book. In bold print, the blurb mentioned that Michigan was Hemingway country. Heikki wasn't sure what that meant but he liked the sound of it, so he drove to his favorite watering hole, the Monte Carlo. He parked his rusty green pickup in front and went in to have a few Old Milwaukees with his friends. He informed them all, in a loud voice, that they were residents of Hemingway country. They wanted to know what that was. "It's a country of the mind!" Heikki told them.

"You're such a bullshitter," one of them replied. Then the conversation turned to the thirty-seven-year-old guy in Misery Bay who had fallen in love with a thirteen-year-old girl. They had dated for a while, had gotten serious, and he had proposed marriage when the girl had barely turned fourteen. The parents had given permission for the wedding but then the county prosecutor had heard about it. The guy ended up in jail, parental permission or no parental permission, and the girl was back in middle school. "I'd throw away the cell key and let the bastard rot," said big Mike Erkkila, who had a niece just turning fourteen.

After a time at the Monte, Heikki drove to the Copper Country Mall. He had never been in the small B. Dalton Bookseller store in the middle of the mall. In fact, he'd been afraid to go in because he knew that, among the profusion of covers and colors, he'd have no idea what to buy. He thought he'd give the place the once-over and see what they had by his new friend and fellow intellectual, Ernest Hemingway.

Heikki noticed right away that the shelved books were alphabetized, so he went to the E section and looked for Ernest Hemingway, but he

19

couldn't find anything. He browsed for a while and came across a book by the overweight TV star Roseanne. The book was entitled *My Life as a Woman*. Heikki remembered that his wife liked to watch that show. It was probably her favorite. He decided to buy her a copy. He carried the book to the girl at the cash register and handed it to her, along with a twenty-dollar bill.

"What's Roseanne doing in Hemingway country?" he asked her.

The girl only smiled, handed Heikki his change and gift wrapped the book in a B. Dalton bag.

Heikki went home. His wife had prepared an anniversary meal of thick slices of boiled tongue, thick slabs of rye bread slathered with butter, and buttermilk. Heikki declined the buttermilk and opened an Old Milwaukee. His wife had put out their best silver and dishes. Heikki felt awkward, so he forked an entire slice of tongue up to his mouth and stuffed it in. He began to chew, and the phone began to ring. Heikki continued to chew while the phone rang a second time. He wondered why his wife had not risen immediately to cross the kitchen and take the phone off its cradle on the wall, but she hadn't.

"Aren't you going to get that?" Heikki asked her, but she took a long sip of coffee strong enough to cause a stroke. She acted oblivious to him and the phone and the undrunk buttermilk. Weeks could pass without a single call for Heikki. Even the companies that called almost daily to promote credit cards or opposing phone companies always asked for Heikki's wife. It was as if Heikki didn't exist.

The phone rang a third time and then a fourth. On the other hand, Heikki's wife got calls all day long—from women friends, church members, relatives, colleagues from the days when she worked, whoever. The phone rang again. Heikki rose from his chair, stormed across the kitchen and grabbed the phone. He shouted into the receiver, "Nobody's home!" and hung up. Then he returned to his seat at the table. "What's the matter?" he asked.

"You've forgotten," his wife said.

"Of course, I haven't," said Heikki. "How could I forget fifty years with you?" Heikki went out to his pickup and soon returned with the B.

Dalton bag, the book safely hidden inside. He handed the package to his wife, who opened it immediately.

"I don't believe it," she said.

"What's the matter?" said Heikki.

"It's wonderful," said his wife. "I never dreamed that you'd buy me a book. Plus, it's about Roseanne. I've been wanting to read this."

"Well, read it then," said Heikki. He finished his beer and chased it with the glass of buttermilk. He wondered if he should kiss his wife, but then thought better of it. He didn't want her to get ideas. Plus, he wanted to eat more boiled tongue. She thanked him for the gift and set it carefully beside her plate. "I was sure you had forgotten or didn't care," she said.

"Of course, I care," said Heikki. "It's just that lately I've been so beside myself that I can't get my attention."

After dinner, the phone rang again, and Heikki's wife began a long conversation with one of her friends. Heikki went outside to the backyard where he discovered his neighbor, Hilda Maki, planting a plum tree just an inch or two on her side of the property line. Hilda had chosen a spot about six feet from the rear corner of Heikki's chicken coop. Years earlier, Heikki had planted raspberries all along the rear wall of that coop, and a straggly patch of raspberries extended out from the coop wall for about five feet. That patch produced about forty half-pints of jam every summer. Hilda's tree threatened Heikki's enjoyment of toast at breakfast.

Heikki walked over and explained to Hilda that, as the tree grew, it would strangle his raspberry plants with its roots. "Plus, the canopy will cut off sunshine," Heikki said.

Naturally, Hilda disagreed. She argued in her small shrill voice that all the roots would stay on her side of the property line and that the tree was clearly just a little thing of no consequence.

My God, the woman makes no sense at all, Heikki thought. "The roots will go wherever they damned well please," he said, beginning to get angry. "And the tree might look small now, but it'll grow to three times its present height very quickly."

Hilda told Heikki he was exaggerating.

"Pretty soon, I won't get enough raspberries from this patch to feed the birds, let alone feed me," Heikki said.

Hilda replied that she might let Heikki have some of the plums that fell on his side of the property line. "I don't want your damned plums!" said Heikki. "I'm a raspberry man." By this, Heikki meant that he ate raspberry jam on his toast every morning and had done so for many years. Hilda could take her plums, he thought, and do something unspeakably perverted with them.

And so the argument continued. While Heikki raved, Hilda watered the little tree, adding a bit of fertilizer to the soil around its base.

"My God! You preen over that tree as if it were Emil's corpse!" said Heikki in disgust. Emil was Hilda's long-dead husband. After Emil had died from a mine cave-in, Hilda had laid her husband's body out on the kitchen table and then had washed it and prepared it for the grave herself. Heikki had helped to bring the body home from the mine and had watched Hilda for a while as she cleaned him up. When she had started to apply make-up to his pale cheeks and flat, gray lips, Heikki had had enough. "Just throw the poor bastard in the ground!" he'd told Hilda, and she'd given him a scathing look. Looking up from applying fertilizer, she gave him a similar look, pulled a long strip of pink ribbon from her apron pocket and tied it around the trunk of the tree.

"Christ! Next you'll be decorating it like a Christmas tree!" said Heikki with disgust, so Hilda pulled a white ribbon out of her pocket and tied that around the tree, too.

Eventually, Heikki got tired and went in the house. He went to bed, but he couldn't sleep. He kept wondering what else Hilda was doing to that tree, out there in the dark, with the mosquitoes and the moon. *And why is she planting that damned tree?* Heikki wondered. Then the answer struck him. Emil had died forty years ago that day. The tree was Hilda's memorial to her husband, to her youth, to her brief time of happiness. *She's been a crotchety old bitch ever since,* Heikki thought. She should have cried when that damned mountain fell on Emil's head and chest, crushing him as thoroughly as if an elephant had stepped on an orange.

22

Heikki remembered the stunned look on Hilda's face when he and the other miners had carried Emil's crushed body into the house and laid it out on the table. Hilda had gone right to work, cleaning him up. Why hadn't she broken down and vented her grief? Even decades after that fall of 1953, she still looked stunned if someone inadvertently mentioned Emil's name. Emil had been Heikki's closest friend, and Heikki had gotten over it. Heikki remembered the pre-war tractor he and Emil used with a cart to haul firewood from the cuttings at the back of their properties. He remembered long-ago Novembers when he and Emil shared a hunting camp out at Rabbit Bay. They had had some great times together. With that thought, Heikki's body dropped precipitously into a deep well of sleep. Outside, the winter's first snow began falling. The Indian summer ended. By morning, the plum tree would be dead, frozen by a brisk northeast wind.

Chapter Three

Hilda

Hilda Maki found herself at a low point in a life that had had no high points since the death of her husband long, long before. In the middle of her long, long bitterness, she had received a chain letter that had been started years earlier by a Catholic priest in the Philippines. Most of the letter was a good luck prayer. Hilda was supposed to make twenty copies of the letter and send these on to other people like herself, who needed some luck. The letter said that if Hilda refused to continue the chain, whether out of spite, forgetfulness, or laziness, she would be punished with terrible calamities. She might even die.

On the very day she received the chain letter, Hilda felt a bit like dying. It was late January, and a blizzard had been engulfing the Copper Country for two days. Before the blizzard, it had snowed every day for weeks, and the sun hadn't shone through the depthless gray skies since December seventeenth.

Hilda had a history of getting cabin fever and acting irrationally every winter, but this particular winter had been worse than usual. The weatherman on the evening news said that they were already approaching three hundred inches of snow. Late at night, every night, Hilda had panic attacks in which she knew, with absolute certainty, that the whole world had been transformed into a gigantic snowball, that she was suffocating at the very center of the ball, and that more and more of the white stuff was being added every second to the outside of it. Hilda lay in bed with the covers over her head and prayed for the snow to go away, but God spited her. Hilda knew she was acting irrationally, and she hated herself for it, but she also hated the whole world, too, because it was out to get her. She knew that Finns were supposed to love winter, but she hated it. She longed for bright skies and song birds.

Then that damned chain letter arrived, threatening to destroy her if she didn't comply with its directions. That letter set something off in Hilda. It made her so mad that she sat down immediately at her typewriter and typed a reply:

BEAT HELL OUT OF SOMEONE YOU DON'T LIKE WHEN YOU GET THIS CHAIN LETTER. IT WON'T HELP, BUT IT'LL MAKE YOU FEEL BETTER UNTIL YOU GET SUED.

This letter has been sent to you by Hilda Maki. I was born and grew up in Misery Bay. I was a moderately ugly-looking girl who grew up to be a moderately plain-looking woman. I have ratty brown hair, a head too large for my body, flat breasts, practically no waist, and legs that look like tree trunks. I have never been very intelligent, have little curiosity, and have always been so dyslexic that my brain sees the last letter in the lower right-hand corner of a page of print when I'm trying to read the first letter at the top left. But since the age of nine, when I finally figured out this dramatic reversal, I read all books from the last letter on each page to the first, and it all comes out right. When I was a girl, I had few social smarts, hence few friends, and was terribly shy. In high school, because I was from a rural area, I was pretty much ignored by everyone. If a teacher could not remember one student's name, it was probably mine. For a while, I had a crush on my social studies teacher, but he paid me no mind. I graduated without ever having had a date. I got a job running the cash register at Coast to Coast Hardware in Hancock. Since then, I have rung up thousands of goods—countless bottles of liquid Draino, cans of basement floor paint, brushes, brooms, and nails. My life had never been anywhere and was going nowhere. So, I began to attend the Lutheran Church. The pastor and congregation were polite but, otherwise, rarely spoke to me. After all, I never had anything to say in reply and often my shyness prevented me from replying. But, inside I was, by then, seething. I more and more felt the need to strike out, to make myself known to others. One day in the middle of ringing up a sale of floor cement, I belted the customer in the face. The customer was a local contractor who had never been hit by anyone, let alone a woman. He was still trying to figure out how to react when I hit him again. A moment later, I had vaulted over the counter and had kicked him half a dozen times in the shin. The customer ran out the door, and I just stood there, feeling wonderful. It was the first time I had felt so good. Then I went back to work and rang up some glue sticks for the next customer. But, for one moment, when I whacked that guy who had done nothing to me, I had felt great! So, send this letter to twenty other people so they can do likewise and feel great, too.

WARNING: THIS LETTER WILL NOT BRING YOU ANY LUCK. IF YOU SEND IT OUT AND KEEP THE CHAIN ALIVE, NOTHING GOOD WILL COME OF IT. ON THE OTHER HAND, IF YOU DON'T SEND IT OUT, YOU WON'T LOSE YOUR JOB, SPOUSE, MONEY, OR GOD'S BLESSINGS. IT WON'T AFFECT WINNING THE LOTTERY ONE WAY OR THE OTHER. IF YOU HAVE A CAR ACCIDENT TODAY OR TOMORROW, THIS LETTER HAD NOTHING TO DO WITH IT. ONE COULD ARGUE THAT YOU SHOULD KEEP THE CHAIN ALIVE FOR THE SENDER, ME, BUT I DON'T EVEN KNOW YOU. So, if you've read this far, stop. This chain letter is a meaningless exercise. Get a life. Please send no money. The chain doesn't work. Nothing works. Life is hell. Poor me. Poor you.

Hilda reread her letter and corrected several small typing errors. Then she put on her coat, wrapped her head in a wool scarf, went outside, and spent two hours shoveling away the huge drift that had built up between her car and the highway. When she reached the road, she spent another half hour punching a hole in the packed and banked snow that the plow had left. Sweaty but energized by the work, Hilda used the arm of her coat and her glove to clear the mounded snow off her car. Then she got in, started it up, waited for a while to warm the engine, backed the car out into the snow-packed highway, and drove to the university in Houghton. There she made twenty copies of her letter on their Xerox machine. It was tax season. Hilda had received her IRS forms just the day before, so she wrote down the two-dollar copying fee on a piece of paper and put it in her pocket. She thought that maybe she could write it off as a business expense.

Back in her car, Hilda drove to the post office and bought a book of stamps. Then she drove to the mall and bought a box of envelopes at K-Mart. She drove back to the university and returned to the library. She asked the librarian, who led her to their collection of phone books. Hilda unshelved the Detroit one and took it to a table where she carefully copied twenty random names and addresses (the odder, the better) onto the blank envelopes. She was relieved by her ingenuity. *No one down there will know who Hilda Maki is*, she thought triumphantly.

Hilda finished her task by sealing the chain letter copies in the envelopes, sealing them and carefully placing stamps in the upper right corners. Then she drove back to the post office and dropped them in the OUT OF TOWN slot. Finished, her body coursed with energy. She felt good for the first time in weeks. She decided to stop at the new Dairy Queen and have a hot fudge sundae before driving home. And when she got home, she'd heat up the sauna and stay in there for a long time until every speck of dirt had leaked out of every pore and her whole body would be clean, inside and out. She'd take a roll in the snow, shower, shampoo and be ready for anything that might come along.

My God, she thought. *Those chain letters really do perform miracles.*

As she drove the lonely miles back to her home in Misery Bay, Hilda remembered again her long-dead husband. *You've been gone over forty years, my love,* she said to him. *You left when I was young. Now I'm an old woman. You wouldn't recognize me. The years have not been kind. I've grown bitter. You wouldn't like me as I am. Worst of all, I've nearly forgotten you.*

Tears formed in Hilda's eyes for her lost youth. Still, she had to admit that she felt better than she had felt in a long time. She really looked forward to a sauna. And, maybe, the next day she'd go skiing along the lake.

Ramsey

Chapter Four

Jackie Puska

Jackie Puska grew to womanhood in the tiny hamlet of Ramsey, Michigan, near the Wisconsin border of the Upper Peninsula. Ramsey had never amounted to much—not even during its heyday as a one-industry mining community early in the century. Then the mines closed, and no new industry replaced them. Most of the population was forced to move. The remaining citizenry commuted to work in nearby Ironwood or found some means to scrabble out an income locally. By the time Jackie was born to a local woodcutter and his wife, Ramsey's main street had been reduced to a long line of boarded up and abandoned businesses. Later still, when Jackie was old enough to commute to high school in Bessemer, the main street resembled Berlin in 1945. The long-abandoned buildings looked as if they had been bombed. The only buildings still in use were Angie's Bar and the Lutheran Church. Angie's Bar was directly across the street from the church, making it convenient for a few of the bar's most avid customers to get there quickly after Sunday morning services ended at noon.

Jackie and her girlfriends talked about getting out of Ramsey at least three or four times a day throughout high school, but they were all small-town girls with a built-in fear of cities. They knew for a fact that every pervert, serial killer, arsonist, and thief not born and brought up in Detroit moved there as soon as he was old enough that authorities could create a permanent record of his felonies. "At least Ramsey is safe and quiet," Jackie used to tell her friend Lillian. "It's the perfect place to marry and raise kids."

"Of course, it's safe," Lillian would reply. "Any place is safe if no one lives there and nothing happens."

At the time seventeen-year-old Jackie was trying to make something happen by spending a lot of time prone in the backseat of Mickey Mustonen's 1956 green Mercury. In 1980, the Mercury sat wheelless and engineless in Mickey's parents' front yard.

Two years earlier, Mickey had bought the rusty hulk for fifty dollars from a junk yard in Ironwood. Mickey planned to rejuvenate the wreck some day and drive it in stock car races where, he was certain, he'd win a lot of money. Every day Mickey lamented his lack of funds for getting the job done. "Jesus raised the dead because it didn't cost nothin'," he liked to say. "On the other hand, raisin' this damned car is costing me a bundle."

Mickey referred to the money he had already spent on engine replacement parts, wiring, a battery, lights, epoxy, primer, a sander, tools, a winch, and lots of other stuff that sat in piles all over the garage floor. The piles had been there for months while Mickey contemplated getting started and his parents contemplated the loss of a parking space for their car. Every day for the past six months, Mickey had assured his parents that he'd soon clear a space large enough for their Dodge. In the meantime, the Dodge sat through the winter in the driveway, where each daily snowstorm buried it anew. Early every morning, Mickey's father had risen to go outside and brush off the night's accumulation while Mickey busied himself in the kitchen, wolfing down huge quantities of bacon and eggs and his mother's homemade *nisu* before he went to work.

Mickey was ten years older than Jackie and worked in the woods. In the winter, Mickey drove to work in a twenty-five-year-old Ford pickup that he'd bought for a song from Eino Pietila. Eino had driven the pickup over a boulder after a night spent in the bars of nearby Ironwood, and the boulder had bent the left front wheel mount. Eino had driven the pickup for several weeks after the accident, but the truck wobbled viciously and threatened to vibrate apart at speeds greater than twenty miles per hour. So, late on a Friday night at Angie's Bar, Eino sold the truck to Mickey. They were both drunk at the time. "Sing me one loud verse of the Kurikka cow-calling song and throw in two hundred bucks and you can have the truck," Eino had told Mickey. "I'm sick of driving that thing. It shakes like a washing machine."

Mickey sang loudly, finishing the song with a flourish by slamming his bottle of Old Milwaukee down on the counter. Then he had passed two hundred dollars to Eino, which was all that he'd been able to save recently for repairs to the Mercury.

In the summer, Mickey drove to work on his motorcycle. He had recently bought new twin Jonsered chain saws on credit and carried them in homemade scabbards on either side of the big black vinyl seat of his Harley. The Harley had been purchased on credit, too.

Mickey had long blond hair embedded with grease. He lumped the hair into a ponytail tied with a black ribbon. He had pale blue eyes as flat and lusterless as a sheep's. Mickey was not tall, not broad shouldered, and not cute, but Jackie liked him anyway. Mostly she liked the thick coat of hair that stretched from his neck to his crotch. She loved to run her fingers through that hair. "A man without any chest hair is as lifeless as the Sahara Desert," she liked to tell her friend Lillian.

Mickey and Jackie had met the night that Jackie had told her parents she was staying overnight at Lillian's. Lillian had told her parents that she was staying overnight at Jackie's. In actuality, the girls planned to stay up all night, wandering the empty streets of Ramsey looking for action. The girls were sitting on the floor in an abandoned store, drinking beer Lillian had sneaked from her dad's cache in the basement refrigerator, when Mickey roared by on his Harley. The girls placed themselves on high alert. Soon they were out in the street waiting for Mickey's return. They knew he would roar past them at some point because Ramsey had only one main street. Twenty minutes later, Mickey returned, and they waved him down and begged for rides. Mickey agreed to accommodate them because he was already two months behind on his bike payments, and if they didn't get a ride then, they might never get one. He thought Jackie was cute, though certainly not in a

conventional way. She had a thin, small face and a tiny frame that empha-
sized skeletal bone. She was also small breasted, thin hipped, and knobby,
but Mickey was taken by the way her straight blonde hair framed her face.
He was especially attracted to the deep blue of her eyes. In her thinness,
Jackie reminded Mickey of his prepubescent sister, and that excited him.

On their final ride that night, Mickey took Jackie to the Mercury in
his parents' front yard, and there they had sex. It was Jackie's first time.
Jackie knew that her parents would be wild if they knew what she was doing
and with whom she did it, so she really enjoyed it.

All through the remainder of Jackie's high school, she and Mickey
were a pair. Then the bank repossessed Mickey's bike and one of his chain
saws, and Mickey's parents told him he could no longer live with them in the
room he'd occupied since birth. They were angry because Mickey had been
spending more time in bars than working in the woods. "We'd rather not do
it this way," Mickey's father told him, "but I guess we're going to have to kick
you out in order to force you to grow up and be responsible."

Mickey put several grocery bags of clothes in the back of his ancient
pickup and put his tape player and heavy metal tapes in the cab. Then he
drove away, leaving his garage-floor piles of parts and tools intact because he
knew that would infuriate his father. "Screw the bastard!" Mickey said aloud
as he drove away, his truck wobbling up the street at fifteen miles per hour.

Mickey drove directly to Molly Erkkila's apartment. Mickey had met
Molly in an Ironwood bar a couple of weeks earlier, and she and he had
immediately hit it off. Mickey was still seeing Jackie, but juggling the two was
not stressful since Molly lived in Ironwood, and Jackie, who didn't have a
car, was confined after school to Ramsey.

Molly was a nineteen-year-old mother of two. She had never been
married. Living off ADC and food stamps, she had a low-income apartment
and a dog named Doink. The other doink was the father of her oldest child.
Whenever the dog got in her way, she kicked it, and the kick invariably
reminded her of the doink who had fathered her child. Then she'd give the
dog another kick, only harder, in remembrance of him. "I hate that son of a
bitch," she'd say.

At first, Jackie didn't believe it when Lillian brought her the news. Then Lillian borrowed her parents' car and drove Jackie past Molly's apartment. Mickey's wobbly pickup sat out front. Jackie recognized every patch of rust, and her fury mounted. "Stop the car and open the trunk!" she demanded.

Lillian drove up the block a short distance, pulled over, and popped the trunk lever.

Jackie was shaking with anger. She pushed open the car door, stepped out, and ran around to the open trunk. She rummaged in the trunk until she found a screwdriver and the jack handle. The jack handle was surprisingly heavy. She walked down the street to Mickey's truck and crouched by the passenger-side wheel. Jackie pushed the screwdriver tip firmly against the side of the tire and then whacked the head hard until the screwdriver burst through the tire lining and air *whooshed* steadily out.

Jackie punctured all four tires, scratched obscene graffiti into the paint of the hood, and then drove a rock through the driver's side window. As the glass exploded into shards, Jackie ran back to Lillian and the car. Jackie glanced back and saw Mickey coming out of the apartment house's front door as she and Lillian sped away.

In the next few months, Jackie went through six boyfriends, two of whom wanted to marry her. The first proposal came from a heroin addict and the second from a drunk. The heroin addict was twice Jackie's age. He had survived for years by suing people for various imaginary faults and injuries. Recently, he had gotten twenty-three thousand dollars from his own auto insurance company after pretending to injure his back in a minor accident in front of a Hancock bar. He'd bought a new Blazer with the money and then used it to force Jackie's recently purchased Escort off the road after he saw her talking to another man. He was very possessive and proposed on the spot in order to ensure that in the future she'd talk to no one but him.

Jackie refused to talk to the addict, locked her car doors, backed up, and drove around his Blazer. The addict leaped onto Jackie's car's hood as she drove away. He pounded on her windshield and shouted curses as the Escort picked up speed. Then the Escort hit a pothole, and the addict fell off.

A few days later, he sued her insurance company for twenty-thousand dollars. Eventually, he got it and never spoke to her again.

The drunk proposed late on a Friday night but had no memory of it by the following morning. "Thank God that he's so stupid that he can't remember," Jackie told Lillian the following day, "because I was so drunk myself that I can't remember whether I said yes or no."

After she graduated high school somewhere near the bottom of the class of 1982, Jackie worked for a while as a bartender at Angie's. Each night after the bar closed, she went off with one of the customers until the early morning hours. Then she crept home to sleep off her hangover until early the following evening. She and her mother fought often over her dissolute life. One of the regular customers at the bar was Matti, an old Finn who had spent his working years in copper mines. His wife had died years earlier. Matti was retired and living alone in a tiny apartment next door to the bar. He came into the bar nearly every night but drank little. He was a talker and seemed to be there to seek out companionship. One night in October of 1983, Matti asked Jackie if she had ever read the *Kalevala*. Jackie had never heard of it. "What kind of a Finn are you?" Matti asked her. "Every Finn should know our national epic."

"I'm not much of a Finn, I guess," admitted Jackie.

"You got that right," said Matti. "All you got is the blonde hair but without the brains." Then Matti went on to explain the part of the *Kalevala* in which Louhi the Witch stole the sun and moon and locked them inside a mountain. "You're like Louhi the Witch," Matti told Jackie, but she didn't understand. "You hang around this damned bar until three o'clock in the morning," Matti told her. "Then you go off somewhere to get drunk and get laid by one of the good-for-nothing bums who hang around this place. You spend every night in such a way that you never see the moon. Afterwards you sleep all day and never see the sun. What kind of life is that? If you keep it up, you'll be an old hag at twenty-five."

Jackie tried to laugh off Matti's words, but he wouldn't let her.

"Just like Louhi, you're a witch," he told her. "But unlike Louhi, you've enchanted yourself. You've stolen the sun and moon from yourself."

Jackie told Matti she was having fun.

"Bullshit," said Matti. "You disgust me—the way you're wasting your life." The old man pushed his nearly full glass of beer away and strode out of the bar.

The next day, Jackie stared in disbelief at the flickering screen of the TV above the bar. The evening news had just begun, and the lead story was about the bombing of the Marine barracks in Beirut. The footage showed dead, dying, and terribly maimed young men. A congressman pronounced the deaths a terrible waste of American lives. "That guy sounds like Matti," Jackie said aloud to no one in particular.

Two days later, the United States led an international invasion of Grenada. Jackie again watched the news in fascination but was most struck by the image of a young American medical student who got down on her hands and knees at some South Carolina air base and kissed the tarmac because she was so happy to be back in America after enduring the upheavals on the tiny island nation. "I'm just happy to be alive," the medical student told the reporter. "Now I want to get on with my life."

Two weeks later, Jackie quit her job at Angie's Bar and left Ramsey. She moved a hundred miles away to Houghton, which she considered a city because it had a population of eight thousand. She found an apartment over the Ambassador Bar and got a job at Burger King. In January, she signed up for an evening business class at nearby Michigan Tech University. She was determined to make something of herself. "One day I want to be someone that my parents can be proud of," she told Lillian during one of their weekly telephone conversations.

Lillian still lived in Ramsey. Lately, she had been dating Doink, the ex-boyfriend of Bonnie Kangas. Bonnie had graduated two years ahead of Jackie and Lillian. Lillian's new beau worked construction in the summer and drew unemployment in the winter. "He barely gets by," Lillian explained to Jackie. "But Bonnie is still always after him about child support. She expects too much. You can't get blood from a turnip."

Years passed. Jackie became the manager at Burger King. Eventually, she became the supervisor of the Michigan Tech University cafeteria. She continued to take business classes in the evenings and during her lunch hour. Eventually, she had taken enough classes to be considered an upper classman. In her senior management class, Jackie had to read a book called *Danger in the Comfort Zone*. It was the first bona fide book that she had read since her Nancy Drew days. Jackie's other business classes had used textbooks consisting of terms in bold print and short, defining paragraphs. *Danger in the Comfort Zone* was full of charts and graphs and procedures that seemed to create order out of the chaos of life. The book talked about empowering managers by making employees do all of the work. The book explained that employees should be valued only for their performance and not for any loyalty the manager felt toward them. The book argued that the workers should compete with each other all the time for employment and that only the most useful ones at any given time should be kept on.

Jackie loved that idea. She was still the manager of the cafeteria, and the idea made her feel powerful—as if she were somebody to be reckoned with. She especially loved the idea of danger at IBM or Burger King.

In her senior year, Jackie read a second book, which was required in a macroeconomics class. The book was called *The Tibetan Way to New Management—Zenning the American Corporation*. The book had been self-published by the class' instructor, who made it required reading for all his students. Jackie could not understand anything in the book. She called Lillian and read her excerpts. "One chapter says I should show the process whereby a sacred cow makes good hamburger," Jackie told her friend. "Another chapter is just called 'How the Path Et Lao,' That's not even good English. And listen to this! 'Yogi Berra says, "When you come to a fork in the road, take it."' Isn't that just nuts?"

Lillian assured Jackie that Yogi Bear never said any such thing. Lillian was the single parent of a six-month-old daughter. She had been divorced from Doink for two months but had yet to receive a single cent in child support from her ex-husband. "Bonnie was right about that bastard," she told Jackie.

Jackie had never been out of the Upper Peninsula, so, to celebrate her graduation from the business program in May of 1990, she decided to visit the Fox River Mall in Green Bay. She'd heard a couple of other women in her classes exclaiming over the shopping. *I'll buy myself a three-piece suit and a briefcase*, she thought. *That way I'll look professional if someone hires me for an executive position.* Jackie thought it was very important to look professional. "After all," she told Lillian when she called her that evening to break the news, "it's not what you know but how you look."

Lillian professed to be envious. "Are you going alone?" Lillian asked. "I'd be terrified of such a big city."

Jackie laughed off Lillian's fear, but the next day she went downtown and bought a road map. She carefully marked off the route in Magic Marker. The store clerk sensed Jackie's fear and gave her detailed directions to the Green Bay mall. "There are motels right across the parking lot," he told her.

Jackie's trip to Green Bay was uneventful, and, after booking herself into a motel, she spent the whole day in the mall. The shopping so exhilarated her that she decided to take in a stock car race advertised on a bulletin board by the mall entrance. She asked directions and found the track on the edge of the city without difficulty. Secretly, she wondered if Mickey Mustonen would be competing. She'd heard through Lillian that he was still single. "He spends practically every night in Angie's Bar," Lillian had told her. "Molly kicked him out. I don't know where he's staying."

As it turned out, Mickey was not competing, but the winner was a cute seventeen-year-old from Iron Mountain in the Upper Peninsula. After the last race was over and most of the crowd had dissipated, Jackie went down onto the dirt track to get the boy's autograph. She was the only fan to approach him, and the boy was shy in her presence. "I never done this before," he said as he penned his name on the back of an old shopping list that Jackie found in the bottom of her pocketbook.

The next morning, Jackie visited the Packer Hall of Fame where she bought a tiny piece of football-shaped plastic with a magnet on the back. When she got back to Houghton, she attached the autograph to the front of her refrigerator with the magnet. She'd forgotten the boy's name and found the signature to be illegible. After a moment, Jackie pulled the signature from under the magnet, rolled it into a ball and threw it into the wastebasket. Then she pulled the magnet from the door and threw it away, too. *I should have bought a football-shaped pin for my new blouse,* she said to herself. *It wouldn't have been so chintzy.*

That summer, Jackie sensed some kind of imminent change. Her life was about to go in a new direction. One evening, she checked the HELP WANTED ads in the paper and discovered that the community college in Ironwood was seeking a part-time business instructor. The position consisted of teaching two introductory classes. It didn't pay much, and benefits were non-existent, but Jackie imagined it could lead to something more. She applied, and when she got the job, she immediately called Lillian, who was too mired in her own problems to be enthusiastic. Her baby daughter had just gotten over the flu. Her ex-husband, Doink, had fled to New Hampshire to work for a builder. He still wasn't paying any child support. Lillian had lost her job as a nurse's aide after her boss received a complaint from a bedridden patient. "But that old biddy complains about all of us," Lillian explained. "I don't see why the boss picked me out as the one to fire." Lillian said that she was going to start tending bar at Angie's the next day.

Jackie had been told that she would teach classes in Business Administration and in Economics in the fall, so she decided to spend part of the summer preparing for the classes by reading *Dilbert*, in the paper. Jackie loved *Dilbert*. She especially liked the pointy-headed boss and the dog. Every day she took notes on what the cartoon could teach her. *Dilbert* could teach her about procedures. If she skipped a meeting in which the procedures were explained, she could open the next meeting by asking for a re-explanation. That way she could waste everybody's time, and nothing would get done. Jackie loved the idea of wasting other people's time. It gave her a feeling of control.

Jackie also saw a relationship between that one book she'd read, *Danger in the Comfort Zone,* and *Dilbert.* In both, the workers lived paranoiacally on the edge of being fired every single day.

Jackie told one of her co-workers at the cafeteria what she was learning from Dilbert. The other woman was shocked. "But *Dilbert* is supposed to be funny. You aren't supposed to take it seriously," said the woman.

"You're such a jokester!" replied Jackie, laughing.

The other woman wanted to know why Jackie thought she'd make a good teacher of business classes. "Because I look nice in a three-piece suit, with a briefcase," said Jackie. "Plus, I love procedures and files and orderliness. I like dotted i's and piles and piles of surveys. Just like *Dilbert*. I've learned a great deal from that cartoon this summer."

The community college in Ironwood was only a few miles from Jackie's parents' home in Ramsey. At the end of August, Jackie left Houghton to stay with her parents while she looked for a place of her own a little closer to the college. Her first night back, Jackie put on a new three-piece suit and went over to Angie's Bar to see Lillian. The same drinkers sat on the same stools they'd occupied years earlier when Jackie had tended bar. "It's as if no time has passed, and nothing has happened," she told Lillian.

"That's Ramsey," said Lillian.

The women hugged and then stepped back to survey each other. Jackie noticed with satisfaction that Lillian had small lines and wrinkles around her mouth and in the faint pouches below her eyes. Plus, she had gained at least fifteen pounds. Neither would be youthful again, but each exclaimed over the changelessness of the other. "You look exactly the same," Lillian told Jackie.

"So do you," Jackie replied.

"But why did you wear the suit?" Lillian wanted to know. "It isn't exactly the kind of outfit seen in Angie's."

"It's intentional," Jackie told her. "I want everyone to know that I don't blend in anymore. I'm going to be a college teacher."

After that, Jackie wandered around the bar, making small talk with former friends and acquaintances. Mickey Mustonen arrived shortly after nine. He'd lost some hair and gained a small paunch, but otherwise, he looked pretty much the same. He greeted Jackie with a hug, as if she were a long-lost friend. He seemed to have forgotten how their relationship ended. When he found out that Jackie was looking for an apartment, he told her to check out Molly Erkkila's old place. "Molly just moved in with Ed Kauppila," Mickey told her. "Do you remember Ed? He works for the county—plowing snow in the winter and repairing potholes in the summer. They've been living together off and on for a couple of years. Molly's got a good man in Ed."

"You and Molly didn't last long," Jackie said, her voice betraying her bitterness.

"Nope. She kicked me out," Mickey admitted. "We were real different anyway. It was all for the best."

"And who are you living off now?" Jackie asked.

Mickey ignored the insult. "I'm back home," he said. "My father died over a year ago. I'm living with my mother. She likes the company."

"Are you working?" Jackie asked.

"Off and on. Mostly off. Ma gets a Social Security check and a percentage of my dad's retirement. We get by. Ma's nearly blind from cataracts. I help her get around."

"He helps her spend those checks, too!" chortled Ted Mattson, a regular at Angie's who was sitting nearby with his ear cocked to their conversation.

"We don't need your lip," replied Mickey.

Ted laughed, a kind of whine that broke off-key. "You in here to put the make on your old girlfriend or to say hello to your new one?" Ted asked Mickey.

Mickey glared at Ted, nodded to Jackie, and then moved to a distant back corner of the bar where he began an urgent conversation with one of his drinking buddies.

"I hate that parasitic bastard," Ted told Jackie. "I tried working with him in the woods. He never did anything but always took more than his share. Now he's robbing his own mother."

Jackie glanced around the bar, trying to guess which woman was Mickey's current flame. She finally asked Ted to identify her.

"Your best friend," Ted replied. "He and Lillian go off together every night after the bar closes."

"I didn't know," said Jackie. She felt a chill running along her scalp and down her back. Her hands began to shake violently, as if they had their own will. Jackie noticed that Lillian had Mickey in the far corner. Lillian was talking quietly with him. Their heads had moved intimately together, their lips no more than an inch apart.

Jackie rushed from the bar out into the night. She felt nauseated. She also felt betrayed—by Lillian, by Mickey, by life. She hated Mickey. How could such a gross man weasel his way into Lillian's life? And how could Lillian have let him? Was she that stupid? And why was she herself back in Ramsey anyway? She should never have come back. She had betrayed herself by returning.

A couple of days later, Jackie moved into Molly Erkkila's old apartment, and before she had properly settled in, classes began.

Jackie's new job was a disaster from the beginning. She really enjoyed looking important as she walked briskly across the campus each morning wearing a three-piece suit and gripping her briefcase firmly in her right hand. But the classes terrified her. She quickly realized that she knew very little about the administration of a business or about economics. She tried to sound knowledgeable about both but kept mispronouncing the big words in the texts. The brightest student was also aggressive and kept correcting her. By October, she ignored the textbooks completely and relied on what she'd read in *Dilbert* and in *Danger in the Comfort Zone*. The students were nearly all from working-class families. Several loudly accused her of being a right-wing conservative. "You're nothing but a Rush Limbaugh stooge," one of the students told her.

Jackie had never listened to Rush's show and wasn't sure what a right-wing conservative was. She felt the students were being unfair, so she repeated the same ideas day after day over and over again. Her twentieth lesson was pretty much the same as her first.

As part of her faculty duties, Jackie had to serve on the Tenure and Promotion Committee. A faculty member who had published a lot of articles and a number of books was seeking a promotion to full professor. Jackie hated the idea that anyone was that far ahead of her. She feared that she would never get anywhere at the college, that every full-time permanent position would soon be filled by someone else. So, Jackie adamantly opposed the candidate's promotion. She insisted to the other members of the committee that his portfolio was inadequate even though it was thirty inches thick and included dozens and dozens of documents. Another committee member pointed out that most portfolios were only one to two inches thick. "And yet they are sufficient," he said.

The other committee members asked Jackie to write down what she felt was inadequate about the portfolio. Jackie did so, but the candidate answered in writing all of her questions.

So, Jackie began to argue that the procedures of the committee had never been adequately addressed. "We need to clarify how we are to work before we can vote on anything," she said several times.

The other committee members became irate because they wanted to move on to other business. "You're a parrot," a faculty member told her. "You repeat points even after the remainder of us have refuted them."

The committee then promoted the candidate over Jackie's protests.

That afternoon, Jackie skipped her class, sat in her car in the parking lot and cried. She knew she didn't fit in the world of academia or of *Dilbert*. She couldn't bear the thought of ever teaching a class again. She seemed to have no control over anything. She couldn't breathe. She felt like she was drowning. She hadn't spoke to Lillian since the night in Angie's Bar. She didn't know if she could ever forgive Lillian for dating Mickey. She hated them both.

The next day, she phoned in sick and then made an appointment with a doctor. The doctor recommended that she take a medical leave of absence from teaching. "You're stressed out," he told her. "You'll make yourself really sick if you continue." He gave Jackie some powerful pills to calm her nerves. She called the school authorities, who agreed to a paid leave for the rest of the semester.

Jackie threw her three-piece suit into a dumpster and drove to Angie's. She and Lillian had a good cry together behind the bar. Lillian had broken up with Mickey the night before. "I couldn't take his laziness anymore," Lillian said between sobs. "He can't even be bothered to clean himself up before we go out."

Jackie told Lillian how much she had hated being a teacher. "These pills the doctor gave me are great, though. I took six for supper, and I feel wonderful. Do you want to try one? They're guaranteed to make you happy."

Both Jackie and Lillian popped a couple of the pills.

"I have no idea what to do," said Jackie. "My life is going nowhere, and nothing is happening."

"Welcome to the club," said Lillian. "Welcome back to Ramsey."

Watton and Toivola

Chapter Five

Santtis

From the late 1800s, various members of the extensive Santti clan periodically emigrated from the lack of opportunity in Finland to the lack of opportunity in Watton, Michigan. Year after year, aunts, uncles, cousins, nieces, nephews, and every other conceivable kind of relation kept arriving in Watton, an Upper Peninsula community so insignificant that the largest business on Main Street was a gravel pit. The second largest was a bait shop. Late in the emigration, a telephone booth was inexplicably set up between the two. Only once or twice in six months did anyone use the phone, but it became the third-largest business anyway, for lack of competition.

The Santtis in Watton were forever writing back to the Santtis still in Finland, begging those left behind to stay put or, if they absolutely had to emigrate to America, to go somewhere else. "There's nothing to do here," they wrote in their letters. "Most of us have to travel quite far to the nearest small towns to take jobs that don't pay much. Some of us work long, hard hours in the forest, but it's difficult to get ahead."

In spite of these letters, more and more Santtis kept arriving. They were a bullheaded lot who didn't believe the letters. "Our relatives in America are just trying to keep all the wealth over there in Watton for themselves," they said to each other. They saved their hard-earned money until they, too, could sail for the promised land. Eventually, the horde of Santtis raised Watton's population to nearly one-half of a thousand.

One of the last members of the Santti family to emigrate was Leena. From her grandmother in Finland, Leena learned to be a midwife and herbalist. She learned the names of hundreds of herbs and their uses. She could brew exotic teas, apply poultices, and weave magic. She knew a dozen uses for burdock plus hundreds of spells good for everything from curing toothache to ensuring good haying days. In Finland, she eventually would have been at the center of the community, a person with special powers. Unfortunately, she chose to migrate to America in 1936, in the middle of the Depression. She thought she was being wise when she chose to avoid Watton. Instead, she went to Detroit because the auto industry had nearly collapsed and virtually everyone was unemployed. In desperation, she thought, they'll seek help through my powers as a wizardess, and I'll get rich. She imagined herself as a kind of good witch for Ford. But, in Detroit, no one was interested in Leena's powers, in part because she had a great deal of trouble being understood. She barely spoke any English, but if they did understand her, Americans merely laughed at Leena's spells. If they had toothache, they went to a dentist, and no one in Detroit was interested in ensuring good haying days. Other Finnish immigrants were no help either. Often they couldn't afford a dentist or a doctor, but they had their own home remedies, usually the same as Leena's.

The only work Leena could find was as a combination charwoman, laundress, and cook in the homes of Detroit's rich. From dawn to after dark six days a week, Leena cooked, washed dishes, scrubbed floors, and did laundry. On her day off, Sunday, she went to the Lutheran church in the morning and then was too tired in the afternoon to do much of anything. She longed to gather medicinal herbs, roots, and berries in back fields, but there were no fields in the city.

Years passed. The Depression finally ended. The world was torn apart by World War II. In Finland, the citizenry went hungry, and its soldiers fought gallantly against the invading Soviet army in the first Winter War. Later came a second war with the Soviets and many skirmishes with Nazi troops. In the meantime, Leena labored on, earning her room and board and little else in the homes of the wealthy. Some of Leena's friends got good-paying jobs in the defense industry, but Leena was held back by her lack of English. She kept up with events, however, by reading Finnish-language newspapers. "Those damned Swedes just sit on their asses while we fight and get killed," she told her friends.

Eventually, the war ended. Leena was losing her youthful spark. Her face had a few wrinkles, and here and there a gray hair sprouted in the midst of the gold ones. The years of hard work had scarred her soul as well as weathered her body. She no longer laughed much. In fact, she had grown very quiet. Her hands were rough and red from constant washing. The skin around her nails cracked.

In America, all around Leena, the post-war boom had begun. Suddenly, everyone seemed to be getting an education. Good jobs with good salaries attached were for the taking. In 1948 at church, Leena met another immigrant, a tall and rather handsome fellow, five years Leena's junior, who had recently emigrated from Helsinki. She and he took long walks together on Sunday afternoons and sometimes returned to his tiny room in a boarding house. The immigrant seemed to be interested in Leena as a woman despite her age and her weathered looks, so she gave herself to him. A couple of months later, she realized she was pregnant. At first the father of the child said that he would marry Leena, but two weeks after that he was gone, and Leena never saw him again. Later, she learned from friends that he already had a wife in Helsinki—a wife he was planning someday to bring to America.

Through the Lutheran pastor, Leena contacted an aunt in the far north of Michigan in Watton. The aunt had not heard about the post-war economic boom. In fact, no one in Watton had. But the aunt was sympathetic to Leena's predicament and invited her to come to Watton to stay with her until the baby was born and until Leena found work. By 1948, Watton was full of Santtis. Santtis had been migrating there for fifty years, and they comprised half of the tiny hamlet. They had all gone there to get rich, but none of them had, and many had already become Americanized and had moved on long before Leena arrived.

In Watton, Leena took any job she could find in the nearby larger towns of Pelkie and Baraga. All of her days became a struggle against poverty and hunger. She still saw herself as possessing special powers, however, and she wanted to instill those powers in her little boy. She believed she could predict the future. "Someday," she told her son when he was yet a preschooler, "you will have a son of your own, and he will grow up to be a great musician, able to weave spells with his music. He will be like the wizard Väinämöinen of our national epic, the *Kalevala*."

The son had heard many stories about Väinämöinen from his mother. She often told him such stories when she put him to bed at night. The son, Dub, liked the idea of having a Väinämöinen in his future family. After all, the wizard had sung his enemies into swamps and had defeated a witch. But the son still found the prophecy strange because neither he nor anyone else in the extended family had ever shown any propensity for music. The boy and his mother sometimes listened to Viola Turpinen's records, and the boy liked the polka music at the Saturday night dances held at the Finnish Farmers' Temperance Hall, but when Leena bought the boy a simple five-string kantele, he ignored it.

In Watton, little Dub was surrounded by relatives. Most lived near each other on back roads, but Dub and Leena lived on Route Two, which passed right through Watton. Watton was so insignificant, however, that the State Highway Department failed to notice it was there and put no signs at either end to slow traffic. Drivers never noticed the place either. They sped right past at sixty-five or seventy, their minds focused on distance and destination. There was nothing remarkable about the few houses buried among the trees off the road. There should have been at least one store, but there wasn't. Mostly there was nothing at all in Watton except trees and Santtis, and most of the Santtis were smart enough to leave. Otherwise, they'd have nothing to do. Dub, however, discovered at an early age that he liked nothing to do. Right from the beginning, he wasn't much of a thinker. He was easily the slowest member of the family. Some of his relatives sometimes joked about it. Dub had unusually long arms, a big chest, a long forehead that sloped back into his brown hair. His face was as gnarled as the root end of a blow down, but it was also flattened out like the end of a sawed log. The flatness was a throwback to Dub's Central Asian forebears. Once in a picture book, Dub saw drawings of an extinct race of beings from one hundred thousand years ago. Dub looked just like one of those drawings.

In Watton, Leena and her son went every Sunday to a small rural Lutheran church where the service was in Finnish. The congregation was made up almost entirely of Santtis. The minister himself was a Santti who had recently arrived from Finland. He was a smug young man who disapproved of almost everything. He saw as his calling the saving of lost souls in the wilds of America. He disapproved of the motives of his congregates. "You people fled the godliness of Finland for the evil of America," he told them periodically, as if he were afraid they'd forget if he didn't constantly repeat himself. "You came here for selfish reasons—to gain wealth on Earth. But God has punished you with Watton. All you have found is endless winters, endless forest, and heathens aplenty." By heathens, the minister meant all Americans who were not Finnish, Lutheran, and Apostolic. He also considered Leena a dangerous and potentially heathen woman because she believed in medicinal herbs, teas, and magic spells. "The only true magic is prayer," he told her and then retold her.

Leena continued to attend the church in spite of the minister because she liked the feeling of peace that the building itself gave her when she sat inside in her usual pew. Also, the services reminded her of her youth in Finland.

Little Dub hated getting up early each Sunday morning in order to go to church where he was bored by the sermon, but he really liked the music. The hymns reminded him of the sound of Leena's voice when she read passages of the *Kalevala* to him in the evening before she sent him off to bed. Dub had seen only two Bibles in his life, his mother's and the big one on the altar in the front of the church. Both were in Finnish. "Does God speak Finnish?" he asked his mother.

"I'm sure he does," said Leena.

"The minister says that our church is the house of God. Does that mean that God is Lutheran?" Dub asked her.

"I'm sure he is," said Leena. "God is in all churches and speaks in all languages. God was in our ancestors when they shaped the world that He had created."

"Did the minister say that?" asked Dub.

"No," replied Leena. "I said that. It's what I believe."

"You make more sense than he does," "Dub said.

When he was old enough, Dub and a couple of cousins were bused to school. The trip was the only part of the school experience that Dub enjoyed. The actual classes were a disaster. Dub was incapable of reading beyond the most rudimentary level, and he considered all math beyond addition and subtraction to be a form of madness. After school, little Dub consoled himself by listening to the radio. It was now the 1950s, and TV had come into existence other places but not in Watton. A very large antenna might pick up one station from Marquette, but the reception was poor, and most folks in Watton, including Leena, opted to continue to discover the outside world through the radio.

Every day Dub listened to the radio drama of late afternoons. His favorite radio character was the Cisco Kid. Dub tried to create a sombrero out of an old straw hat he found on a nail in the barn. He affected a sort of Mexican accent twisted grotesquely by Dub's Finnish accent. One of Dub's uncles, who himself spoke with a very thick Finnish accent, took to calling his nephew the Sisko Kiid. Dub's other uncles and aunts had harsher terms for the boy. They called him simple or slow or dumb.

The year Dub entered high school, the telephone booth between the gravel pit and the bait shop became a post office drop box. Stamped letters went into a locked box with a slot, which hung on the side of the booth. Any larger packages with correct postage could be left inside the booth. The booth's walls were decorated with postal regulations and a single FBI poster of a wanted fugitive from San Diego. Hanging on the back wall was a small stamp vending machine. In his junior year, Dub dropped out of school and went to work in the woods with an uncle with a logging truck. The uncle felled and limbed the trees with a chain saw while Dub piled the limbs out of the way. Dub also used a tired old horse named Blackie to drag the logs to the roadside with a chain. After the uncle cut the logs into four-foot lengths, he and Dub loaded the logs onto the truck bed by hand, the two working together to lift and shove the heavier stump ends on first. Once they had a load, the uncle drove the truck to the mill while Dub napped in the passenger seat. At the mill, they climbed onto the top of the logs and quickly unloaded. Then they returned to the woods to complete the whole process again. They usually finished a second trip to the mill just before it closed. Then they returned to the woods to fell, limb, drag and pile wood until it was too dark to see.

Dub loved the work. It was outside, and he didn't have to take orders from anyone except his uncle. Dub liked the smell of the forest and of freshly sawn wood. Plus, the work was almost purely physical. Dub didn't have to think very much, and he liked that. He especially liked sitting on a stump during a break and sharing a beer with his uncle. But just after Dub's eighteenth birthday, the uncle ruptured a disc in his back and could no longer lift anything. He had no insurance and delayed getting an operation. Instead, he trucked loads for other loggers, and Dub rode along to load and unload.

Six months later, Dub was drafted into the Army, went through boot camp, went through truck-driver training, and was sent to Vietnam. In 'Nam, he mostly trucked supplies from one base to another. The work was tedious and not once did his truck come under attack. He could just as well have been trucking back in Michigan for all that he saw of the war. He began to smoke dope and drink heavily. In off hours, he frequented the whore houses that ringed the base. He re-upped for a second tour, still saw no action, and returned to Watton at the end of his second tour—a conquering hero in a snazzy uniform. At one time or another during his two years in 'Nam, Dub had caught every venereal disease known to man, but the Army doctors had cleaned him up, and shortly after his return home, he began a serious courtship of a girl from L'Anse. Dub got back into logging, and within a year, he and the girl from L'Anse were married. She was Finnish, too, and Dub assumed she would fit right into the world of the Santtis.

All of Dub's relatives joined in to build Dub and his new bride a log home in Watton. "I don't want to live here," the bride insisted. "There's nothing here." She wanted to live in a real town with a real post office, a supermarket, and some shops. But, after the crowds and noise of Asia, Dub loved the absolute silence of Watton. Plus, changes were occurring. The telephone booth between the gravel pit and the bait shop was now a conduit to the Baraga County Sheriff's Department. All a person had to do was to pick up the red phone inside the booth, and he or she was automatically and instantly connected to the dispatcher at the sheriff's office. "It's just like the president's hotline to Moscow," argued Dub.

In the next few years, Dub became a successful logger with his own truck and other expensive logging equipment. He liked the long, hard hours out in the woods. In fact, he greatly preferred working to being at home. He didn't know what to do with his wife. He loved having sex with her, but, beyond that, what was a guy supposed to do with a woman? They had children—five of them, three daughters and twin sons. When Dub finally came home from work, he expected peace and quiet and a pliant wife, but what he got was the noise created by little children and a wife who was tired. In frustration, Dub spent night after night in bars, leaving his wife a kind of prisoner in their log home in Watton.

When the oldest daughter was in first grade and the twin boys were barely one, Dub's wife left him for another man. "I'm sick of Watton, and I'm sick of you!" she shouted at Dub as she disappeared out the door.

Leena moved into the log home and took over the job of raising the children. She had had a prophetic dream the night before. In the dream, one of Dub's tiny twin sons was eating the eyes out of the fish head used to make soup. "It's a sign," Leena told Dub. "One of your sons is privileged. A special guest at the table gets the eyes." Leena told Dub that one day soon, he would have to move the family. "One of the twins is destined to become a singer of epics, a Väinämöinen," she told him. "If he's going to become famous, he ought to be raised in a bigger town closer to the paths to power—a town where his special powers can be recognized."

Of the twin boys, Eino and Uuki, Leena was certain that Uuki was the destined one. "All the signs are there," Leena pointed out. "He looks like a Finnish hero, with his blond hair, blue eyes, and broad shoulders. Plus, he

58

loves smoked fish and everything pickled—beets, herring, eggs, sausage. For breakfast, he gobbles up blood sausage and blood pancakes. He likes dill on everything. Even his eating habits are heroic. Those are the foods of the Gods."

"For a little kid, he's quite a glutton," said Dub.

Dub put off moving for a while. The 1980s had arrived, and a few enterprising people in nearby towns were making huge profits from renting video tapes. Dub decided to open Watton's first video outlet in the telephone booth by the gravel pit. He put in shelving for several dozen tapes and hired a nephew as an attendant, but the nephew quit after one day. "It's like spending all evening in a coffin," he told Dub.

The next day, a niece worked at the booth, but she complained about the cold and also quit. Then Dub tried to go without an attendant. He left a sign-up sheet in the booth. Customers were supposed to write down their name and the name of the rented tape. Then they were supposed to put the rental fee into an empty coffee can. Somebody stole all the tapes and the can.

Like most people with little education and little intelligence, Dub was easily bored. A new Indian casino had opened in Baraga, and Dub began to spend a lot of time there. He liked to drink at the bar, play the slot machines and wander around trying to pick up women. After he'd gotten courage from a lot of drinks, Dub always used the same pickup line on every woman: "Hey, you wanna take a ride with me?"

Occasionally, he succeeded because the casino attracted women with empty lives who were desperate for any kind of attention. But one night a very beautiful young woman many years Dub's junior agreed to go for a ride with him. Dub could hardly believe his luck. He and the woman parked by Lake Superior for a while in Dub's van. They talked about their families. The woman was married, with several young children, including a sick baby boy that her husband was caring for at home. "The baby just wouldn't stop crying," the woman told Dub. "He's been sick for a couple of days, and his crying was really getting on my nerves. I had to be alone—away from husband, kids, everybody. That's why I came over here. It's an addiction. I love to gamble, but I usually lose three or four hundred dollars."

Dub asked the woman how often she gambled. "Every week," she replied.

After a while, they kissed, and the rest of the night rushed by in a blur. The young woman did things to Dub that his wife had never done, and Dub knew, by the time he dropped the woman off at her car so that she could drive back to her family in an unknown small town, that he was in love. It didn't work out. A week later, in the casino parking lot, Dub asked the woman to leave her husband. The woman laughed. "You've got to be kidding," she told Dub. "I could never live in Watton. There's no there there. You're an attractive guy in a very rough sort of way, but we'd never have anything to talk about. Apparently you don't read, and you've never traveled except to Vietnam, where you were drunk all the time. I like you, but you're a bore. Plus, you have a family to raise, and so do I. It would never work."

Dub and the woman met clandestinely a number of times after that, usually late at night when the woman had lost a lot of money on the slot machines. Then her husband became suspicious, things got messy, and the woman disappeared out of Dub's life forever.

For a while, she continued to call him at odd times. Dub wanted to call her back, but he didn't have her number and didn't know her name. Plus, he suspected that most of what she had told him was a lie. She had changed the stories about her children several times. He had told her a lot about his life, but she had revealed little about herself. He wondered if she even had a husband or made him up to use as an excuse.

The night the woman told Dub that he'd never see her again, Dub got raving drunk. He sat at the casino bar for hours, overwhelmed by a sense of loss and hopelessness. Of course he had his mother and the kids, but something essential was still missing in his life. He tried to figure out what it was, but the alcohol made the room whirl, and he ended up shouting incoherently at somebody on a nearby barstool. Near dawn, he made it home and collapsed in his bed. He woke up sometime later in a panic. The house was still, but Dub could not shake the idea that he was buried alive in a box six feet underground. Starkly awake, he could still smell the dank decay of the freshly mixed earth. The weight of it sat lumpishly on his chest, making it impossible to breathe. When Dub tried to get out of bed, panic overwhelmed him, and he fell to his hands and knees and crawled to the bathroom where he retched again and again into the steaming bowl. Still, the panic would not leave him. He knew he was going to die. Death would be a relief. On his hands and knees, like a dog, he crawled down the stairs and out the front door. The sun was just coming up, but a few stars still shone in the west. Dub lay on his back on moist grass and looked up at them, at their indifference. *A thousand years from now*, he thought, *no one will remember that I logged, that I lived and breathed and felt a breeze on my face.* He suddenly realized what Leena had been trying to tell him for years. The only salvation was through song, he realized. *The Kalevala will live forever, but we are temporary.*

The family moved to a run-down farm in Toivola, a rural hamlet only fifteen miles from the twin towns of Houghton and Hancock. Hancock was the unofficial capital of Finnish America. Its seven thousand inhabitants were nearly all Finns. Toivola was also Finnish and resembled Watton. It was so small that its entire business district consisted of a shed for the town plow, a bar (the Mosquito Inn), and a combination gas station/diner. At breakfast and lunch, the diner was the social center of the town. People congregated there to gossip and to eat pasties— fat turnovers filled with ground meat and finely chopped potato, rutabaga, carrot, and onion. Toivola folks sometimes argued fervently and loudly over the proportion of these ingredients and whether or not some of them should even be in the recipe.

Leena was now an old lady with arthritis, but that hadn't slowed her down. She still bustled about the house, maintaining order and cleanliness. Right from Uuki's birth, she had watched for signs that he would be a wizard someday, a singer of such power that his fame would ring down through the ages. She noted when he was a baby that he often sang "Three Blind Mice" in his bath. She noted that he yowled as if in rhapsody when Viola Turpinen sang on Leena's old Victrola. He bounced about the kitchen on his short, chubby baby legs when a polka played on the radio.

In fact, the signs of Uuki's extraordinary nature were there right from the beginning. Uuki was a superhuman daredevil from a very young age. He was the child who smashed up two Radio Flyers, demolished several trikes, knocked the wheels off several dozen toy trucks, knocked the heads off dolls, broke the pieces to innumerable games, and generally left the entire family periodically toyless. Uuki was not vicious in his destructiveness. He was just incapable of controlling his wildest impulses. If he suddenly felt the need to swing from the highest branch of a sugar maple, he did so. It really wasn't his fault when his hands slipped and he fell, bouncing from limb to limb until he struck the ground, breaking an arm and a leg. Even for Uuki, that fall was pretty dramatic. Usually he merely skinned his knees or his forehead or his elbows, the fall also shredding the cloth of jeans or shirt sleeves. By the time he was five, Uuki had stepped on so many nails that his father made jokes about it. "If I'd've left all the nails in," he told men with whom he worked, "that kid's feet would resemble porcupine tails."

Uuki's destructiveness drove Dub crazy, but Leena saw it as another sign that the boy was extraordinary. "He has no use for the common things of this world," she told Dub after Uuki beheaded his sister's Barbie doll with a pair of kitchen scissors. Leena admired the way the boy managed to start the lawn mower when he was only five and then pushed it down a long row of vegetables in the garden, neatly slicing off the tops. Leena put a positive light on Uuki's insistence that he always get his own way. "He's been set apart from the rest of us by his destiny," Leena explained to Dub.

"Set apart, hell! He's just spoiled rotten and naturally unruly," insisted Dub.

Uuki was never one to come in second, especially with his brothers and sisters. He was extremely competitive with his twin brother, Eino. If Eino blew a bubble with his stick of bubble gum, Uuki had to blow a bigger one with two sticks. If Leena or Dub bought Uuki and Eino identical new tennis shoes at K-Mart, Uuki always demanded a more expensive pair for himself. If Eino had a friend over to play on Tuesday, Uuki had to have two friends over on Wednesday. If Eino had a medium-sized potato at supper, Uuki wanted one that was at least slightly larger. Of course, Uuki's competitiveness caused constant fights between the boys, and then Leena would intervene. "Leave your brother alone!" their grandmother would shout. Their father would threaten to tan Uuki's hide.

At bedtime, Uuki would dawdle, always brushing his teeth after the others. Then he would hang around downstairs after the others were already in bed. Every night, Leena would tell Uuki multiple times that he had to get to bed. Every night, he resisted until one or the other started shouting. "Ninety percent of the tension in this house is caused by that kid!" Dub frequently said.

Uuki was almost always the first child in the family to try something that they all knew was forbidden. He took up smoking in the fifth grade. He stole a carton of his dad's cigarettes and hid them on a beam in the hayloft of the barn. Then he stole a box of matches out of the kitchen and climbed into the barn loft to try out tobacco. Eino, who followed his brother into the hayloft, tried to dissuade his brother, but, of course, Uuki wouldn't listen.

In fact, his brother's bantering persuaded Uuki to smoke more. He lit the first cigarette and puffed on it as hard and as fast as he could. As soon as it was finished, he lit another and continued to puff hard and fast. By the tenth cigarette, Uuki was feeling woozy. "You'd better save the rest for another day," urged Eino.

In reply, Uuki lit another, took a puff, looked surprised, leaned suddenly forward and vomited. When his body finally stopped heaving, Uuki looked with disgust at the lit cigarette in his hand and then tossed it away from himself. It landed in the dry hay, and within seconds tall flames raced through the hay toward the dry timber of the barn walls.

"Let's get out of here!" cried Uuki.

He and Eino slid down the ladder and ran out of the barn and across the yard toward home. Leena was in the kitchen at the back of the house. Uuki and Eino went upstairs to their room. They sat down on their bed and began playing a game as if nothing had happened.

"Dad's going to kill you," said Eino.

"No, he won't," said Uuki.

"You just burned down the barn. It's burning down right now."

"Maybe he won't notice," said Uuki.

As soon as Dub returned home from delivering a load of cordwood to the mill, he noticed that the barn was gone. Nothing but a smoldering black square remained. The family had lost two cows, a dozen hens, a goat, lots of tools, and an old truck in the fire. That night, the fire chief came out to look at the remains. Dub asked the chief how it might have started. "These things are often a mystery," said the chief.

"There's your mystery," said Dub, pointing toward Uuki, who stood on the other side of the yard, trying to look innocent.

"You don't know that," said the chief.

And, of course, Dub didn't. The cause of the fire remained a family mystery.

Uuki was also the first Santti kid to drink. He and the others attended a one-room schoolhouse called the Heikkinen School. During the morning recess in the spring of Uuki's sixth grade, he sneaked off through the woods and broke into a neighboring home owned by the Virtanens. He didn't really break in because nobody in Toivola ever locked a door. He just walked in, found nobody home, and began to rummage around in the kitchen cupboards. He told Eino later that he was just looking for something to eat because he'd gotten up too late that morning to eat breakfast. On the top shelf of the cupboard above the sink, he spotted a nearly full fifth of mint vodka. He pulled over a chair and used it to stand on the rim of the sink. From there he was able to reach the bottle. Sitting on the kitchen table with his legs dangling over the side, he drank all of the vodka straight from the bottle. At first, the vodka was the worst-tasting stuff he'd ever put in his mouth, even worse than the worms he'd eaten on a dare in the schoolyard with all the other kids watching. The last few slugs of vodka, however, tasted really good. Uuki tried to put the empty vodka bottle back on the shelf over the sink, but he nearly fell off the chair and dropped the bottle. It shattered in the sink. He turned on the water full force and ran the glass splinters into the disposal. Then he turned on the disposal and was amazed by the noises it made.

Uuki remembered how hungry he was. Again he rummaged through the cupboards and brought some Saltines and Skippy to the table. He also found a knife but was so drunk that he smeared most of the peanut butter on the sideboard instead of on the crackers. He left his mess on the table, crawled under it, and passed out.

That's where Mrs. Virtanen found him when, hours later, she returned home from her job as a secretary at Northern Hardwoods. By then, Uuki's teacher was frantic, Leena and Dub were frantic, and the sheriff's department was organizing a search through the woods. Everyone feared that Uuki had wandered off and accidentally drowned or a tree had fallen on him or he had been eaten by a bear or a cougar. A cougar had been seen in the neighborhood months earlier, and people remembered. Bears, of course, were always around.

When Uuki got home, his dad tanned his backside with such fury that he sprained his wrist. He had to take a couple of days off because he couldn't lift anything.

While Dub waited for his wrist to strengthen, he took a trip back to Watton to see his old haunts. He drove slowly past the gravel pit, noting that it had grown very little since his move to Toivola. The bait shop now also sold bakery. Its sign advertised the selling of freshly baked *nisu* and night crawlers. Dub parked his van in front of the MICHIGAN BELL TELEPHONE BARAGA COUNTY SHERIFF'S DEPARTMENT HOTLINE UNITED STATES POST OFFICE PACKAGE/LETTER DROP BOX VIDEO RENTALS EMPORIUM booth and noted with satisfaction that his part of the sign, though now a bit ragged and faded, was still there on the door. Dub left his van, entered the booth and called Leena. "Guess where I'm calling from," he said when she answered.

In junior high, Uuki often played hooky in the spring in order to fish one of the many small trout streams behind the family property. Sometimes Eino would go with him, but usually Uuki wanted to be alone. He liked to spend a day by himself, communing with nature and escaping the boredom of school and the internecine jealousies of the school cliques. Uuki would trundle off into the woods with his pole, a creel, a bottle of fly dope, a tobacco can full of worms, and a cap with dry flies hooked into its band. In his pack pocket, he usually also carried a couple of cherry bombs and a book of matches. He only used the cherry bombs when the fish refused to bite. Then he'd light the large firecracker and toss it into the center of a pool where he was certain trout lurked. Immediately after the explosion, the stunned fish would float to the surface. Uuki would wade in and retrieve them before they came to their senses.

When he returned to the house, Uuki would clean the brookies and toss the offal into the bushes at the back of the yard or would feed the entrails to one of the cats. At suppertime, Leena would roll the beautiful stippled little fish in cornmeal and fry them in a thin pool of bubbling butter until the skins were crisp and the meat was a juicy pale pink. Eating the brookies was one of the great joys of Uuki's life.

In fall, Uuki frequently skipped school to hunt. He especially loved to wander the back fields of abandoned farms that dotted Toivola. Their forsaken orchards were prime feeding grounds for partridge, the occasional pheasant or woodcock, and rabbits. Sometimes Uuki would stealthily enter an orchard, raise his shotgun, and blast away at the trees with birdshot just for the hell of it. He liked bringing down on his own head a thick shower of applewood branches, twigs, and leaves while a covey of partridge whirred loudly away. Other times, he brought home a brace of partridge and a couple of rabbits, which Leena would turn into a thick stew with dumplings.

Uuki was never much interested in stalking deer through the forest during crisp fall days, but he greatly enjoyed night hunting when the deer came out to feed by a road or in roadside fields. Uuki liked to freeze them in the beam of a jack light and then shoot them while they stood befuddled. Such kills never had to be dragged very far and never required much walking on Uuki's part. Leena strongly disapproved of such illegal activity, but Dub didn't seem to care. "The venison tastes the same," he insisted.

In the fall that Uuki entered high school, Dub caught his leg under a falling tree and broke it in three places. He managed to crawl to his truck and drive for help, but he was laid up for weeks while the leg healed. During that time, he encouraged Uuki to hunt every day. "All of that free meat will cut down on our food bills," he told Leena.

While Uuki hunted and the other children were at school, Dub sat stationary on a chair by the kitchen table and within reach of the beer in the refrigerator. His injured leg with its cast was propped on another chair in front of him. Dub sat there each day for hours with a beer in one hand and a cigarette in the other. Whenever a fly landed on the table or on the wet top of the beer can, Dub would fry it with the lighted end of the cigarette.

In high school, Uuki was even less interested in school subjects than he had been previously. He pretty much ignored math altogether and didn't do much in English or history either. He hated science. He was quickly streamed into the remedial classes for dummies. He never read an entire book on his own. He started one or two by Louis L'Amour but never finished them. His dislike of reading caused dissension with his brother. Eino was the sort who couldn't live without books. He read or tried to read all of the time. He would keep a book handy in his jacket pocket when he was out in a blizzard shoveling snow. During the long winter nights, he often read for hours up in the room he shared with Uuki while Uuki sat in the living room watching TV with the rest of the family. One evening when Leena and the girls were in town shopping and Dub was out in the yard trying to repair a broken hydraulic rod on the plow, Eino and Uuki sat alone in the living room. Uuki was watching a Road Runner cartoon, while Eino was reading a lay person's guide to Einstein's Theory of Relativity. Intellectually excited by what he was reading, Eino tried to explain some of Einstein's ideas to Uuki. Without a word, Uuki rose from where he was sitting, walked across the room and struck Eino squarely in the face with his closed fist. Blood streamed from Eino's broken nose.

At Jeffers High School, Uuki hung out with the drop-out types. Some of them formed a rock band. Since the band members couldn't read, write, or do math, the band was their way of gaining recognition and respect from their peers. The band was their way of being counted. Music had never been important to Uuki, but he began to listen to Kiss, Metallica, Aerosmith, and the Dead Kennedys. He especially liked the Dead Kennedys and Jello Biafra. Uuki bought a Walkman and wore his headphones much of each day. Leena was excited by Uuki's sudden interest in music. "Soon he will fulfill his destiny," she told Dub. That Christmas Leena bought Uuki a full-sized kantele. Dub, who liked the music of Patsy Cline and Ray Price, urged his son to learn to play the instrument.

"What the patrons need at the Mosquito Inn, the Range Lounge, the Loading Zone, and the Monte Carlo is less rock and roll and more traditional Finnish music," Dub told his son.

When Uuki balked at the idea of playing a Finnish harp, Dub urged the boy to think about adding a whole new element to the local music scene. "Maybe you could combine Finnish traditional music with current American music. Why not join together country and the kantele? You could call your band the Kantele Cowboys."

Feeling like a fool, Uuki brought his kantele to the rock band's practice sessions in Joe Maki's garage. Joe's parents didn't let them play in the house because they made such a racket, so the boys had rigged up a space heater in the garage and played there for hours. To his surprise, Uuki was welcomed into the group, along with his kantele, but it soon became apparent to everybody except Uuki that he had no musical ability whatsoever. No matter how long he practiced at home and in Joe's garage, he still could not hit the right notes. At first the other band members were embarrassed by Uuki's ineptitude, but soon they realized that if the drummer drummed ferociously, the electric guitarist strummed viciously, the key boardist whacked the keys melodramatically, and the vocalist sang as loudly as possible, no one could hear the kantele anyway. And so everything turned out all right.

Sometimes the drummer's sister would hang around while the band practiced. Kathy Pyhtila was sixteen, and the first time that Uuki saw her, he knew he was in love. He was too shy to speak to her, however, so he wrote her a song. The first line went like this: "When I fell in love with the drummer's sister." The second line said, "I fell all the way." The rest of the lines were pretty much the same. The band added the song to the rest of its repertoire, which was made up entirely of punk and heavy metal pieces from various bands.

Eventually, the band got its first engagement—at a nursing home in Houghton. The audience consisted of a couple of dozen deaf or nearly deaf old ladies and a couple of old men. The audience smiled and clapped politely after each piece.

For a few months, the band booked the Toivola plow shed every Saturday night and played. They set up between two plows and in front of a big mound of mixed dirt and salt for throwing on icy roads. They charged a dollar to anyone who wanted to come into the shed to listen to them or to dance. A lot of young people showed up every Saturday, not because they liked the band but because there was nothing else to do in Toivola.

After they graduated from Jeffers High School (or, in Uuki's case, dropped out in the middle of his senior year), the band members continued to get together to play. At first they were invited to play only at high school dances, but eventually they became a part of the local bar scene. They had a gig every Saturday night in one of the local drinking holes. They played all over the Keweenaw and seemed to be everyone's favorite local hard rock band. They even pooled their money and paid for a recording. They sold a lot of copies, too. People bought them at the dances or in local music outlets.

Then, on a Saturday night at the Uphill 41 Club, a drunk approached the band, waved wildly for them to stop playing, and grabbed one of the mikes. "I can't hear the guy on the kantele," the drunk shouted into the microphone. "I want to hear him play."

The Uphill 41 Club was crowded that night with lots of rowdy college students, most of whom had never heard of a kantele. But they began to shout, too. "The kantele! The kantele!" they chanted. "We want to hear the kantele!"

And, so, Uuki had his first solo performance. When the room quieted down, he tried to sing his own composition about falling in love with the drummer's sister, but he found it impossible to play and sing at the same time. He plucked the wrong strings or failed to pluck them altogether. Then he forgot the words and hummed for a while. He was so nervous that his voice cracked, sounding like fingernails on a blackboard.

When Uuki finished, everyone in the bar cheered wildly. They loved his playing because it was so excruciatingly awful. "More!" they shouted. But that night there was no more. The band returned to playing their renditions of various hard rock songs and Uuki's kantele was once again drowned out by the other instruments.

Uuki's performance on that Saturday became legendary. Word of his horrendous musical inability spread rapidly among the local young crowd, and, after that, every time the band had a gig, some drunk would shout for

Uuki and his kantele. Uuki liked the attention and misunderstood the crowd's enthusiasm. He thought they really admired his playing. He composed more songs. One was about a copper miner's daughter. Another was about Keweenaw guys and what they liked. The first line of that one went like this: "Keweenaw guys like to hunt and fish and drive old cars." The second line said, "And they like to hang out in local bars." The rest of the song was pretty much the same.

As Uuki's popularity grew, the band began to set aside time for Uuki to solo every time they performed. Dub came to one of these performances at the Range Lounge, and he was so taken by the crowd's enthusiasm for his son's playing that he offered to pay for Uuki to record. "We'll make a million when you get national recognition," Dub told his son.

Dub took a couple of days off from logging, and he and Uuki drove for ten hours south to Detroit. It was the first time either had crossed the Mackinac Bridge. In Detroit, Dub used the family's savings to pay for the recording session and to pay for a thousand copies. The sound engineer kept complaining about the low point which Motown had come to, but Dub and Uuki ignored him. When the thousand copies were ready, Dub and Uuki stacked them in the back of their van and then drove around Detroit, visiting radio stations, meeting disc jockeys, and giving each a copy of Uuki's music. They drove all night to return to the Keweenaw, where Uuki's reputation as a horrible musician continued to grow. People bought tapes of his music to give to their enemies or as joke gifts to cheer up the hospitalized. A Hancock Lutheran pastor played it as background music when he sermonized about Hell.

Leena listened to the recording and decided there was something seriously wrong with it. If people liked his playing so much, as Dub said was the case, she wondered if maybe he wasn't so bad. She decided to go to one of his performances.

On a frigid Saturday night in January, Leena and Dub drove through a blizzard to hear Uuki play at a bar in Houghton. They got there early so they could sit right by the band. "I don't want to miss a single note," Leena told Dub.

When the band began to play, the music was so loud that Leena thought she was in an earthquake. The walls vibrated out of focus, and the air itself took on the thickness of water and rushed at Leena in waves. She gasped and tried desperately to hear Uuki's kantele, but all she heard was a wall of sound rushing out of half a dozen huge speakers right in front of her. She felt a magic power in the music. It was like Väinämöinen at his angriest, and she, too, like Väinämöinen's enemies, was being sung into a swamp. The bar's filthy floor seemed to rise up to smash into Leena's face. "The music, the music!" she cried out, but no one could hear her. She pitched sideways off her chair and fell face forward onto the floor. The music was suffocating her. She gasped for air but choked on the noise.

Dub dropped to the floor beside his mother and then waved his arms wildly for help. The music stopped. Dub checked for Leena's pulse and put his cheek close to Leena's open mouth to see if he could feel her breath. She was dead. Dub rose to his feet, his face ashen and shouted for an ambulance.

Uuki still sat, frozen with horror, behind his kantele. Dub pointed his arm accusingly toward the band, his body now shaking with fury. "Your damned music killed her!" he cried. "She's been killed by rock and roll!"

From that moment, Uuki never played the kantele again. He quit the band, married Kathy Pyhtila, went to work at Northern Hardwoods, began to drink too much, smoked pot nearly every evening, got divorced, remarried, had a son, got divorced again, and shuffled back and forth among various single-parent moms who were afraid of commitment.

After his mother's death, Dub began to spend nearly every night drinking and gambling at the casino in Baraga and yearning for another woman to walk into his life. He began to put on weight. He gambled himself so deeply into debt that he lost his logging truck and skidder to the bank but still owed a huge sum to the IRS. He died two years later of a massive stroke while sitting at a slot machine. He had put forty dollars into the machine when he died, and he had built up ten credits. The casino board debated sending flowers to the funeral of such a good customer, but then they voted against it because of the expense.

71

Uuki's sisters married hard-working local guys, had kids, and settled into common lives.

Eino graduated from Northern Michigan University with high honors in literature, went on to get an M.A. in Literature from the University of Michigan, returned to the Upper Peninsula to work for a while in a print shop in Hancock, and settled in Ontonagon, where he sold insurance and enthused about Dostoevsky.

Disc jockeys in Detroit played Uuki's music on April Fool's Day, and listeners loved its awfulness, so disc jockeys continued to play it, usually introducing it with a joke. Recently Uuki's music was released nationally by a major recording company. Uuki sometimes gets satirical fan mail from as far away as Germany and Hawaii. He doesn't answer any of it. Mostly, he works Monday through Friday at Northern Hardwoods and hangs out on weekends with whichever single-parent mom he's temporarily living with. His fame grows slowly but steadily.

Misery Bay

Chapter Six

Arvo Salonen

The dirt road that led to Arvo Salonen's boyhood home was on the left off the Misery Bay Road, about five miles beyond the tiny hamlet of Toivola in northernmost Michigan by the south shore of Lake Superior. Although the road had no sign, locals called it Salonen Avenue since no one but Salonens had ever lived on it. Salonen Avenue was just wide enough for two vehicles to pass. In spring, it turned into an impassable mud bog, and in summer great clouds of dust rolled out behind any vehicles that rumbled down its pot-holed surface. The road progressed straight on through scrub forest for nearly a mile, then dead-ended at a turnaround.

The road had been hacked out of the forest by Arvo's grandfather shortly after he arrived unwillingly in America in 1918. The grandfather had used primitive tools and brute strength to build the road. The larger trees had been felled with a saw, the smaller ones with an ax. The limbs had been dragged by horse and chain to the side of the road. There the logs were cut in manageable lengths and piled. Some were used for firewood, but the majority were sold. The grandfather extracted the massive roots by digging under them, then wedging a crowbar underneath and throwing his shoulder and entire weight against it. He usually had to do this multiple times from multiple angles before he had created enough space below the main rootball to wedge in a log or two. Then he jimmied a chain underneath and around the root, hooked it to the horse's drag bar and let the animal do the rest. With especially troublesome roots, he used a pick and spade to tunnel underneath. He would then wedge a stick of dynamite as deep in the hole as he could place it, light the fuse, run back and drop behind a nearby tree to listen to the roar of the explosion, then the buzz of debris. This often was followed by the *whunk* of the root as it settled. Then he came out, wrapped the softened root in chain and let the horse work. The upturned roots were dragged to the lake side of the road to form a windbreak. The whole process was tedious. So was the building of the primitive log cabin that became his home during his first Michigan winter. The floor was dirt, the chinking was dirt and bark with spruce sap for glue. The roof was rough hand-hewn lumber covered with tarpaper. The corners of the cabin were true ninety-degree angles. He was proud of those corners and the tight way the logs locked together.

Thirteen years earlier, when Arvo's grandfather was a boy of twelve in Finland in 1905, his twenty-year-old brother had been forcibly drafted into the tsar's army to fight in Russian's war against Japan. The brother had died in the Far East. The widower father, who had been in poor health for some time, could not handle the farm work alone. He slipped quickly into debt. In 1908 he lost the farm. Wealthy neighbors bought the land cheaply and expelled the family. The father died a broken man, and Arvo's grandfather and his siblings had hired on wherever they could find work. Arvo's grandfather became a tenant on what used to be his father's land. The new owners thought they were doing him a favor when they gave him a plot to farm, but by then he hated the provincial class system and the tsarist government. In the evening, by candlelight, he read the ideas of Lenin and other socialists and became a follower. In 1918 when civil war broke out in Finland hard on the heels of the Russian Revolution, Arvo's grandfather openly proclaimed his Communist sympathies and became a small-time commissar. He and other socialists burned the homes of white sympathizers. Several enemies of the Party were shot in the village, and others had to flee to Sweden. The grandfather himself arrested a local schoolteacher and the road commissioner. Later, there were mock trials, and both were shot.

When the tide turned in 1918 and the whites won the civil war, Arvo's grandfather suddenly found himself a wanted man. If he were caught by the whites, he, too, would be proclaimed an enemy of the state and shot. Before fleeing to America, he stole at rifle point a small nest egg from wealthy landowners in his village. With that money, he bought passage for Michigan. With more of the money, he bought the forest land in Misery Bay and built the road. His experiences in the civil war had left him embittered and paranoiac. He wished to live far from neighbors, at the center of his own property surrounded by a wall of forest. He never cleared fields for hay or other crops but did build what he called a farmhouse, with an attached barn, and there he lived alone. The farmhouse was a considerable distance beyond the turnaround and could be reached only by a path that wound through the woods. In winter, the grandfather skied from the turnaround to the house.

Arvo's grandfather successfully avoided neighbors, never learned more than the most rudimentary English, and made his living alone in the forest, felling trees with the same age-old tools that his father and his father's father had used in Finland. In 1923, he advertised for a wife in a Finnish newspaper. The woman who answered had long dreamed of going to America. She had seen pictures of America's Midwest, where farms were huge and the soil was unbelievably rich. She had heard stories of the wealth to be gained there. She checked on a map and noticed that Michigan was in the Midwest. She surmised that Misery Bay had to look like those Indiana and Iowa farmlands.

Arvo's grandfather paid his bride's passage from Finland and married her in the Lutheran Church in Toivola as soon as she arrived, disoriented, in that little hamlet. He then brought her to the farmhouse in the forest. Upon arrival, she complained that there was no farmland, only forest. In answer, he showed her the small garden plot behind the barn.

Inside the house, the bride rushed from room to room, inspecting his handiwork. "What kind of man would build a house without a single closet?" she asked him as they returned to the primitive kitchen with its sink that drained through the wall into the yard. There was a well but no running water, lamps but no electricity, hooks but no closets.

Soon he learned that his new wife was a frugal, hard-working, God-fearing Lutheran who had never missed a Sunday service in her life. He, on the other hand, was an atheistic socialist who dabbled in the occult and was prone to talk about out-of-body experiences. From that first day, their marriage was a war. They agreed on nothing. If she said they'd have peas for supper, he'd say they'd have corn. She hated the way she had to sneak off to church in order to avoid his many belittling statements about the delusions of ministers. "Jesus was a homosexual," he told her many times. "That's why he hung out with the twelve disciples."

On the other hand, he hated how she prayed for him when he tried to talk about the coming new world order and the triumph of the proletariat.

They had a son, Arvo's father-to-be, in 1924, but his arrival simply increased their bickering. The father wanted his son to be pro-union and anti-government. "Don't trust anyone but socialists," he told the boy. "America will be a great country when it joins the Soviet Union in the new world order." He taught the boy to sing the *Internationale* and union songs.

The mother urged her son to be pro-church and respectful of the country that had taken her in. "Put your faith in God," he told him. "Pray for God's forgiveness for your father's sins."

In the fall of 1929, the mother caught a persistent pneumonia that would not be conquered. She lingered on, barely alive, into 1930. Every breath sliced through her congested lungs, causing her to gasp with pain. That January, blizzard followed blizzard until the whole world seemed to be drowning in white. The mother lay abed, covered with quilts while the wind swirled around the house and made the walls shake. Day after day, she and her son prayed that she might get well and return to life, but her condition worsened. About three weeks before her death, she had a revelation and gave up on prayer. "I talked to God," she told her son in between bouts of coughing and gasping. "He wants me to forcefully return to life by rejoining the living."

But she was too weak to get out of bed. She was wracked with fever and hated the cry of the wind as it encircled the building, driving more and

78

more snow before it. She would have to return to life from a distance. When her husband brought her a supper of cabbage soup and rye bread, she attempted to sing one of his favorite pro-union songs. He was astounded and wasn't sure if she was being sarcastic or honest. She tried to explain the change in her by saying that she had been reborn again at the point of death. God had given her a kind of unspiritual revelation. Removal from life through prayer meant removal from life altogether. Immersion in life meant staying with the living. "I want to see my son grow up!" she told her husband, her voice full of desperation.

During those last three weeks, as her life ebbed away and her breath became shorter and shorter, she forced herself to seem happier than she had ever been. She hummed the Internationale whenever her husband was around and told her son that she now looked forward to the coming Communist utopia. "But, in my utopia, God will be there," she told her son. "For workers like me, the sun will shine warmly every day, birds will sing, and flowers will grow profusely all around the foundation of this bleak farmhouse." In February she died in her sleep.

Her son grew to manhood in the isolation of the forest and under the tutelage of his reclusive father. At home the boy and his dad spoke only Finnish. At school, the boy spoke Finnglish in the early grades but spoke something that was clearly a form of English by the third grade.

The father taught the son to hate capitalists, which the boy translated into a dislike of Republicans. The father taught the boy to hate cops, lawyers, and bureaucrats, which the boy translated into minor acts of rebellion at school. Though the boy remained painfully shy and oddly mute through elementary school, he was intelligent and polite and did well despite an almost complete lack of social smarts.

The boy did most of his growing during the Great Depression. From the time he was a little child, the father taught the boy survival skills. In elementary school, he already knew the niceties of running a trap line. He cleaned the traps himself and boiled them for hours to rid them of any vestige of human odor that might cling to them. He skied into the woods on homemade skis that his father had hewn and shaped out of rough boards out in the barn. He concealed the traps along stream banks, wherever he saw animal signs. He caught mink, otter, and the occasional lynx. He sometimes killed the frantic animals with a sharp blow to the head with a weighted club he carried in a pack on his back. Other times, he shot them in the head with a .22 pistol. He then carried the carcasses a considerable distance into the woods, skinned them out, and used parts of the remains to reset the traps. The rest he scattered.

The boy became an excellent hunter and fisherman. He and his father built deer traps on the back of their property and baited these with apples, beets, and unneeded seed potatoes. The boy trapped bear and grew fond of the rich, dark meat. He fished streams and ponds, bringing perch, trout, walleye, hornpout, and other fish to the table.

In the home, the boy performed most of the necessities. He cleaned with a frayed broom and a graying mop. He dusted with greasy rags. He washed dishes. He chopped firewood. He disposed of hot ashes. He did laundry in a tub, using water heated in buckets on top of the stove. He hung the laundry outside winter and summer. In winter, when he brought in the clothes as the sun set, they were stiff as boards and made crunching and popping noises as he folded them. The boy became a decent cook. His specialty was a fish stew called *kalamojakka*. The father and the boy pickled their own herring and salted their own salmon and trout. Together they cut venison and bear into thin strips and dried it into jerky. The father was a good teacher of survival skills when he wasn't in the woods felling and limbing trees.

In free moments, the boy read Western and detective magazines and books from the school library. The father looked at this reading material with disdain. "Read something useful," he urged the boy. The father read socialist tracts and a socialist newspaper published in Finnish in Superior, Wisconsin.

At the beginning of September in 1939, the boy began high school in Painesdale on the same morning that Hitler's forces attacked Poland and World War II began in Europe. Arvo's grandfather read about the Russo-German Mutual Defense Pact in the Finnish Socialist paper from Superior.

He was horrified. Soon Soviet forces attached Finland, and the Winter War began.

Arvo's grandfather kept his son out of school the day of the Soviet invasion of the old country. He lectured the boy on betrayal and told him that loyalty was one of the most important attributes that a man could have. "But don't carry that loyalty beyond your own family," he told the boy. "Never trust a government. Stalin has betrayed his own people and the Party, and his people are so stupid that they've betrayed themselves by fighting his wars for him."

While the boy watched in silence, his father gathered up a stack of the socialist newspapers from a corner of the kitchen. He had intended on rereading them on winter days when inclement weather made it impossible to work outside. He threw the entire stack into the stove and burned them. Then he got down on his knees and began to pray. The boy was considerably baffled. When he finished praying, the father explained his actions to his son. "To hell with the proletariat," he said to the boy. "All over the world people are acting stupid. They're letting themselves be used by capitalists and dictators. I've shifted loyalties to the God of the forest, wind, and river. On Sunday, we'll pay homage to the Power in Nature by taking a walk in the woods or by going fishing or hunting."

From that moment, the father became a backwoods anarchist. He became even more reclusive. He often went all day without speaking. The boy was happy to escape the silence for the socializing at school.

At the high school in Painesdale, he invariably wore a gutting knife in a sheath on his belt, a flannel shirt with frayed elbows, and a scuffed and misshapen felt hat with fishhooks embedded in the band. He found himself accepted by his peers anyway, primarily because he could do things with a basketball that they couldn't.

He became a guard on the basketball team, and for the first time, girls were interested in him. One of the cheerleaders, a Manninen from Atlantic Mine, asked him to take her to a dance, and from then on, they were a couple. She was a stereotypical cheerleader—cute, perky, and dumb. In high school, she labored through arithmetic while he took algebra and physics. She took home economics while he took chemistry and advanced English. After graduation, they married and were almost immediately separated by World War II. While his dad was in the Pacific, Arvo was born. A year later, while Arvo's dad was still in the Pacific, his half-sister was born. The sister's father was a French-Canadian from Lake Linden. Arvo's mother had met him at the movies. The French-Canadian was ineligible for military service because he had lost an eye during a boyhood collision with a limb when he fell out of an apple tree. The French-Canadian had hated losing the eye until he realized that the loss made him the only young man available to lots of lonely young women whose husbands and boyfriends were off to war.

In the Pacific, Arvo's dad was wounded twice—once by a sniper's bullet that sheared off the middle toe of his left foot as he dove headfirst into a shell crater and once by dozens of tiny fragments from an exploding shell. He was hospitalized multiple times for swelling in the legs and undiagnosed jungle fevers. Healthy or not, every week he wrote faithfully to his wife and father. He received only one reply from his father, who wrote in Finnish to tell him that if he should die, his death would be senseless. "This world war, just as was the case with the first one, is capitalists fighting capitalists," the man wrote.

In the summer of 1945, Arvo's dad finally received a letter from his wife. It was written in the large, round letters of a child, with lots of common words misspelled. "If anyone rites that I met a boy from Lake Linden at the moveis and that weve been seeing each other stedily, they're lying," she wrote. "I never met such a boy!!" She never mentioned the recent birth of her daughter.

When Arvo's dad returned home in late 1945, he discovered for the first time that he was the father of someone else's child. He never completely forgave his wife for her indiscretion, but he tried hard not to blame the child. From that moment, he and his wife were not exactly at war; it was more like an endless fencing match with each opponent constantly parrying the verbal thrusts of the other. The daily tension was exhausting but manageable. They lived in an apartment in South Range, and Arvo's dad ran an auto body shop until 1950. That year, Arvo's grandfather died, and they moved into the farmhouse at Misery Bay. As a moving-in present, Arvo's father bought his wife a green formica table and matching chairs for the kitchen.

It didn't help. His wife hated the primitiveness of the place. Without electricity, the farmhouse lacked most amenities. There was no refrigerator and only an old-fashioned wood-burning stove. Music and news came only from a battery-powered radio on a kitchen shelf. The faint glow from kerosene lamps made it impossible to read after dark. She tried but got headaches. The smell of the burning kerosene offended her nose and the invisible soot from the burning wood plugged up her sinuses. But her husband was quite content to live as if the present were the past. "Except for your constant nagging, it's peaceful," he argued.

Foods that needed to stay cold were kept on shelves in a kind of earthen closet or root cellar built into the back of the cellar. Water was pumped out of the well by an old-fashioned hand pump at the sink. The sink drained into the yard. There was a hand-powered washing machine, so she went into town to do the laundry at a laundromat.

Her husband spent an inordinate amount of time making wood or piling it or carrying it into the house or carting out the ashes in two large buckets. She wanted to replace the two wood stoves downstairs (in the kitchen and living room) and the small oil heater in the bedroom with an oil furnace, but the oil truck could not go beyond the dead-end turnaround in winter, and its extended hose would not reach within several hundred yards of the house.

"An oil furnace! With all this wood around? I never before heard of such a dumb idea!" said her husband.

Arvo's dad quit his job at the body shop and began to work in the woods, as his father had done. He logged the land he had inherited and leased other properties. He made a down payment on his own logging truck, bought a second-hand bulldozer and an ancient tractor. He owned several chain saws. He was reasonably successful, but the home was full of anger. Arvo's mother hated the farmhouse isolation, lack of insulation and overall roughness. Arvo's dad added on two rooms and closets and put on new siding, but she wasn't satisfied. "This isn't my house," she often said. "It will never be my house. It's your parents' house and yours. I'm an outsider."

Arvo's mother also hated Misery Bay, and the neighbors lived too far away. "I need to live in a real town," she often said. She hated the cars they drove. "I deserve at least a Buick or an Oldsmobile," she said. "Not just a common Ford or a Chevrolet." She hated not having enough money to buy whatever she felt like buying on a whim. "Why should I have to figure out if we can afford it," she often asked.

Arvo's dad worked from dawn to dark and often later. His wife could not stand to be alone in the house all day. Although her husband urged her to get a job and get out of the house, she refused. "Why should I work? I'm not a man. We pay the bills." She accused her husband of trying to take away her freedom.

Each day after he went off to work, she drove the ten or so miles to South Range to check the mail. Then she'd return home. Soon, she'd need cigarettes and return to South Range to get a pack. Then she'd return home but would soon need ice cream and would once again drive to town. Sometimes she'd drive to town seven or eight times in one day. Her restlessness made her a kind of joke among the neighbors. The women remembered her affair with the Lake Linden French-Canadian during the war, and they worried about their own husbands. The husbands referred to Arvo's mother as "that restless bitch." They wondered why Arvo's father still kept her around. "She must be good in bed," they surmised. "Otherwise any self-respecting man would have kicked her out a long time ago."

Arvo had no problems with his mother. He was close to her and to his father. His father taught him the same survival skills that he had learned as a boy. Summer and winter, Arvo was often outside. He hunted partridge with a shotgun, rabbits with a .22, and deer with a Savage. He stream-fished for trout and pond-fished for anything that would bite his hook. In winter he fished through the ice. He never learned to trap. By then, most of the fur-bearing animals were scarce.

From his Depression-era father, Arvo learned to be frugal and hard working. He learned to distrust the government, especially the Department of Natural Resources. He learned to scoff at cops and lawyers and all bureaucrats. He learned to be independent and self-reliant.

Arvo read widely from the time he was a boy, was an excellent student at Jeffers High School and went on to get a two-year degree at Suomi College in Hancock. Almost immediately after he finished at Suomi, he was drafted into the Army and a few months later found himself in Vietnam. In the dank heat of midsummer in 1966, his company was cut to ribbons in a two-day-long firefight near the Cambodian border.

In 1967 Arvo left the Army, returned home, enrolled at Northern Michigan University and became a history teacher. For several years, he taught downstate, and then Arvo's former history teacher at Jeffers retired early, and Arvo replaced him in 1970.

In 1972 Arvo's father's logging truck lost its brakes coming down Bridge Street in Houghton. The truck crossed two streets, an embankment, and a small parking lot without hitting anything and plunged into the Portage Canal. The impact caused the chains holding the logs to snap, and the logs hurled forward, crushing the cab and trapping Arvo's father inside, where he drowned.

After the funeral, Arvo's mother left the farmhouse that she despised and moved to Marquette where, as she put it, she could enjoy the benefits of a big city. Arvo inherited the farm and moved back into his boyhood home.

Years passed. Arvo continued to live alone privately, frugally, and self-reliantly. Month after month, he banked most of his checks. He did repairs on the farm himself. Much of his food came from the land. He ignored game seasons and took deer, bear, 'coons, rabbits, squirrels, partridge, and a variety of fish whenever the opportunity presented itself. In spring, he gathered fiddlehead ferns along the flood banks of the Misery and Sturgeon rivers. He canned dandelion and mustard greens and scoured the forest for edible mushrooms. He bought his clothes at second-hand stores in Houghton and Hancock. He drove rusty junkers already near the end of their lives, purchasing them for a few hundred dollars. He drove them until they needed serious repairs. Then he abandoned them somewhere on his property, usually between the farm and the turnaround. Sometimes in a single year, four or five of these clunkers were added to the metal carcasses scattered about the farm. Arvo planned to sell the lot to a junk dealer someday. In the meantime, he cannibalized them for parts. He insisted that the wrecks were like money in the bank. "Someday some junk dealer will give me good money for all that metal," he told other teachers at Jeffers High School.

Arvo became eccentric in other ways. He read in a magazine that Scottish deer hounds were one of the rarest breeds of dog in the world. He drove all the way to Vermont to purchase a male and female pup from a breeder. He dreamed that the dogs would make him rich. "There are only a few hundred of these dogs in the whole world," he told his teaching colleagues. "If they ever become popular again, I'll be able to sell them for a huge sum. They're like money in the bank."

Arvo liked to purchase off-beat magazines on his occasional trips to Houghton. On one trip, he purchased an antique car magazine. He assumed that the magazine was about the kinds of cars he had abandoned all over the farm. He was amazed that they had a magazine for clunkers like that, but when he opened the pages he found that the articles concerned much older and much more expensive cars. In the ads in the back, a man from Wisconsin was trying to get rid of a 1940s vintage twelve-cylinder Lincoln. Arvo called the man, discovered that the car didn't run and needed lots of repair. Arvo drove to Wisconsin, met the car's owner, bought the car, and paid to have it towed to Misery Bay, where he parked it at the turnaround. Arvo loved the old Lincoln. "There's more metal in that Lincoln's bumper than there is in a whole car today," he told other teachers.

Sometimes Arvo would sit for an hour or two in the dead Lincoln and dream of cruising the highways and byways of America in the gigantic car. *Boy, could I pick up women in this car if it ran*, he thought. He liked rubbing his hand over the burnished surface of the teak-colored dash. He loved to peer through the yellow-tinted glass at the dials with their dark-red needles. He loved to open and close the glove compartment, which was so large that he could easily fit a lunchbox inside, with plenty of room left over for maps, a flashlight, or a box of Kleenex. He loved the fact that the massive doors swung smoothly and silently open at a light touch when the car sat on level ground. He loved the immense trunk and the even larger back seat. *Wow!* he thought. *I could do unspeakable things back there and have room left over for a party.*

From the middle of December to the middle of April, two to three hundred inches of snow fell on Arvo's road, and, as the snow piled up along the road banks, the plowman found it more and more difficult to keep the road open. At the turnaround, the plow's blade buried the ancient Lincoln by the first week in January, and, after that, as the banks grew almost daily from new snowfall, the plowman found it more and more difficult to turn around the plow. He mentioned his problem to Arvo. "You hauled that damned wreck all the way from Wisconsin to the end of this road. Why didn't you haul it twenty more feet so it would be off the road?"

Arvo pointed out that the carcasses of clunkers lined the edge of the turnaround. When the plowman then pointed out that the Lincoln hadn't run in forty years and was just another clunker, Arvo took offense. He argued that the hulk was an antique and worth its weight in gold.

As the years passed, Arvo grew lonelier and lonelier but also ever shier around women. He compensated for his shyness by treating women with clumsy formality. He often removed his hat in their presence but then didn't know quite what to do with it. He fumbled with it or twirled it on his finger or dropped it. In their presence, he spoke nonsense, becoming master of the obvious. "It certainly is snowing," he would say in midwinter when it had been snowing every day for two weeks. Or he would point out that it was cold in January. He made horrible mistakes. One morning in the faculty lounge, the woman who taught typing broke one of her nails and asked if anyone had some nail clippers. Arvo handed her his hunting knife with the six-inch blade.

Arvo continued to live very frugally. Decade after decade, he banked the majority of his checks. He thought sometimes of taking a trip to Europe or Tahiti or even North Dakota or nearby Canada, but he couldn't bring himself to spend money in such a foolish way. It wasn't that he ever worried about not having enough money. It was just that spending any large sum of money felt like a betrayal of his dead Depression-era father.

Then, in the fall of 1985, Tiltu appeared in the back row of Arvo's senior American History class. In 1985 Arvo was forty-three, Tiltu seventeen. Tiltu was thin and tall and stunningly beautiful, with long blonde hair, bright gray eyes, and an explosive laugh that seemed to carry Arvo right down inside her. Tiltu had quite a history before she entered Arvo's history class. That history began with her name. Her drunken father had named his newborn daughter after the Finnish version of Tokyo Rose. Moscow Tiltu had broadcast out of the Soviet Union in the fall of 1939, urging Finns to betray their government and to lay down their arms for the heroic Red Army. When Tiltu's father sobered up and realized what he had done, he said, "The name seemed a good idea at the time." For a while, he meant to go through the process necessary to get it changed, but he never got around to it, and after a while, the name stuck.

Tiltu also had a sexual history. Just down the street from her childhood home in Hubbell was a plant, run by the university in Houghton, that produced copper wire. A middle-aged married man did after-hours general clean-up there. He flirted with her as she walked by with friends. Later, she returned to the plant alone, and he introduced her to sex. She was barely fourteen, but she immediately loved it. She was too young and naïve to realize that the man was abusing her, that she was being used. Instead, she understood that she was using him to discover forbidden adult pleasures.

Tiltu went back several times a week for over a month, but then a neighbor told Tiltu's mother that something was going on. Tiltu's mother confronted the man and threatened to have him jailed. Tiltu watched from behind some bushes. She saw panic and fear on the grown man's face and then heard him crying. She discovered the power of her sexuality.

After that, she still met the man a couple of times, but his wife found out, and he wouldn't see Tiltu anymore. Tiltu ended the relationship by pouring sugar into the gas tank of his truck and then slashing the truck's tires.

Because of the affair, Tiltu's family moved to a new home in Atlantic Mine, and Tiltu attended school in a new district. Tiltu's home life was chaotic, and the move did nothing to change that. Her father worked steadily and hard for an electrical company, but on weekends, he invariably drank himself into a frenzy and attacked his wife. He accused her of having multiple affairs with all sorts of unlikely men—an old man who had lost an eye in World War II and who walked with a limp, a thirty-three-year-old retarded man who lived with his parents, the wall-eyed cousin of a neighbor, the older brother of the paperboy. Sometimes the mother goaded her husband because his violence made her feel morally superior. When Tiltu's father came after his wife with his fists and feet, striking her hard in the head and stomach, knocking her down and kicking her as hard as he could, Tiltu invariably came to her rescue. She sometimes leaped onto her father's back, wrapping her left arm around his neck and pulling his hair with her right. Other times, she threw herself between her father's fists and her mother. The father always stopped. He never hit his child.

When Tiltu was a high school sophomore, her father got a job eighty miles away at the White Pine mine. Her parents decided to move, but Tiltu didn't want to lose her new school and friends. One day in September, right after the bus dropped her off at her home, she walked the short distance to the main highway, stuck out her thumb and caught a ride westward. Her third ride was with a trucker going to Duluth. He threatened to return her to her parents, but she made up an exaggerated story about abuse, in which her father physically assaulted her with his fists.

In Duluth, the trucker stopped at a motel and took Tiltu to eat at a diner. "We'll stay in the motel tonight," the trucker told her. "In the morning, I'll decide what to do with you."

In the middle of the night, Tiltu slid into the trucker's bed and showed him a good time. Afterwards, she glared at him menacingly. "Now you're not going to tell anybody about me," she told him.

Before dawn, she slipped out of bed, dressed in the bathroom, stole two hundred dollars from the trucker's wallet and left. She walked five miles out of town to a truck stop and caught a ride to Fargo.

Later, she traveled southward and eventually arrived at a commune in the Arizona desert and stayed there two months, living with a group called the Family. Her commune boyfriend preached the occult power of pyramids and ate only green vegetables and grains. He rode a really nice Harley that Tiltu liked very much.

The week before Christmas, Tiltu called her parents. They sent bus fare, and she returned home. They hadn't moved after all. Her father still worked at his old job.

In her junior year, Tiltu became a fringe member of an Upper Peninsula motorcycle gang whose members came from all over but who met each weekend at a prearranged site. A black-jacketed gang member would pick up Tiltu from her home on a Saturday morning. For the rest of the weekend, she would take long rides with them into Wisconsin or to the Lower Peninsula.

As a senior, when Tiltu was a student in Arvo's American History class, Tiltu met a twenty-seven-year-old motorcyclist from Misery Bay who worked on cars. She moved in with him, and they were together until Tiltu's mother left her alcoholic husband, took the six other kids (all younger than Tiltu) and fled to a trailer that a friend owned as a hunting camp in Misery Bay, not far from Arvo's farm. Tiltu moved back in with her mother to help with the rearing of the younger children. Because Tiltu lacked a car and because the motorcyclist was busy working, Arvo volunteered to drive her to school every day. Soon Tiltu had begun a sexual relationship with Arvo, but she didn't like him much. She thought he had strong body odor, and he was not physically attractive. His hair was thinning, his skin had roughened with time, and his hands were large and coarse. Plus, he had all those junk cars all around his place, and Tiltu hated that kind of disorder. On the other hand, on one of her visits to his farm, she noted his bank book sitting on the table, opened it, and found out how much money he had stashed away. What she mostly liked about having sex with one of her teachers was the realization that she had power over an authority figure.

Although he was too shy to say so, Arvo was obviously in love with her. It showed in the way he dropped things in her presence—a glass of wine, his hat, his grade sheet during class.

In March, Tiltu moved back in with her motorcyclist, but in April she spent a weekend with Arvo at the farm. When the motorcyclist found out, he was frantic. There was a confrontation, but the making up was sweet, and the pain in the motorcyclist's eyes gave Tiltu an odd kind of pleasure. She saw the same pain in Arvo's eyes at school, and so her pleasure doubled.

For some years after Tiltu graduated, Arvo did not see her. He knew she was working at a fast-food restaurant in Houghton but he never went in there. In the meantime, Tiltu found out she was pregnant. She quickly aborted the child because she knew she had no future with the motorcyclist. He was not educated, would never have any money, and could never give her security. She continued to live with him until she was twenty-three, however. By then he was sick of her frequent tantrums and her occasional affairs, so he left her for the steadiness of Annukka, a quiet, trustworthy girl who had been in Tiltu's high school class. After the break-up, Tiltu poured sugar into the gas tank of the motorcyclist's Harley and slashed the tires on Annukka's Toyota.

Tiltu started spending a lot of time in bars and collected a string of boyfriends. Benjamin was from downstate, was intelligent and was a graduate student in civil engineering at Michigan Tech. Don was a cocaine addict from Calumet who lived off the insurance companies of people he sued for various imaginary accidents. When he sued Tiltu, she broke up with him. The Latvian was from the south side of Chicago and did drug counseling at a Houghton clinic, but he smoked pot daily and grew his own marijuana under infrared lighting in the attic of his home in Hancock.

On an October afternoon, Tiltu came face to face with Arvo in the parking lot at the Copper Country Mall. She flirted outrageously, and he responded, as she knew he would. He took off his hat, stuttered, spoke in incomplete sentences, blushed, fiddled with the hat, dropped it and stumbled when he bent to retrieve it. Tiltu had always looked for sophistication in her boyfriends, but she never had found any. She hated clumsy, ill-mannered people. And, here was Arvo, so clumsy that he couldn't even hold onto his hat. He fit smoothly into the backwoods world of Misery Bay, but he would look like an idiot in a place like New York. Still, he had all that money in the bank. Tiltu considered that. She also gave some thought to the idea that she might just be able to reform him.

In 1988, Arvo and Tiltu married. She was already pregnant but happy. Arvo made more money than most men made in the Copper Country, and he liked to polka. He talked about traveling. For years he had been interested as a historian in the Finnish diaspora. He wanted to visit distant communities where a substantial percentage of the citizens were of Finnish heritage—Monson and South Paris in Maine, Fitchburg in Massachusetts, Fairport Harbor and Ashtabula in Ohio, Lake Worth in Florida, Cloquet in Minnesota, Lake Norden in the Dakotas, Butte in Montana, Negaunee over near Marquette.

Tiltu wanted to travel, too, but she thought Avro's destinations seemed foolish. She would much rather take a Caribbean cruise or visit Disneyland, the Mall of America near Minneapolis, Minnesota, Lambeau Field and the Packer Hall of Fame in Green Bay, Wisconsin, or some other place of similar sophistication. Arvo wasn't interested. "I'd rather see downtown Negaunee," he said.

Tiltu wanted to find a nice home in town and move into it. She knew Arvo could afford such a move, but he was adamant about continuing to live at the farm in Misery Bay. Tiltu hated the idea of being so isolated, and she hated the way the brooding forest came practically up to both the front and back doors of the farmhouse.

"I'll live here at the farm, but I'm going to change some things," Tiltu told Arvo. "And someday soon I want to live in town. We could sell this place and use the money for a better house. This land must be worth a lot."

Tiltu washed everything in the house after she moved in and then papered, painted and laid down tile. After considerable haranguing, she got her name added to Arvo's bank accounts. then she spent his money on new plumbing, a completely new bathroom with a large, deep tub, and a new kitchen with double sinks and lots of cupboard and pantry space. She called the power company and got electricity poles and lines run out to the property. She hired an electrician to install outlets in every room. In a matter of weeks, the farmhouse was brought into the twentieth century. Tiltu bought an electric range and refrigerator for the kitchen and a TV, CD player/radio, and humidifier for the living room. She bought a series of appliances: a bread maker, a coffee maker, an ice cream maker, a toaster, a blender, a dehydrator, an electric wok, a microwave oven, a slow cooker, a washer and dryer. She had phones installed in the kitchen and their bedroom.

Arvo found himself overwhelmed by the rapidity of change. He considered all the new things to be a waste of money. "We don't need any of this stuff," he said.

In answer, Tiltu dragged the green formica table out of the house, lugged it across the yard and tossed it into the woods. She followed the table with the chairs. then she drove into town and bought a new table and chairs made entirely out of bird's-eye maple.

Arvo tried to protest. "My mother bought that formica table," he told Tiltu.

"In the fifties," she returned.

"It's still as good as new," he said.

"We'll see what a few winters do to it out there in the woods," Tiltu said.

When Tiltu finished with renovating the house, she set to work on the barn. She tossed the butter churn into the woods and ordered Arvo to slaughter the laying hens, the rooster, and the rabbits. "We can buy chicken and eggs at the supermarket," she said. "They're cheap. And I don't like rabbit."

Arvo had large bags of coarse salt lying around. He used this to preserve the meat of the animals he shot. The rich smell from the bags revolted Tiltu. She tossed the bags into the woods. "With a refrigerator, you won't need to dry and salt meat," she said.

Then Tiltu transformed their bedroom into a kind of pink palace, with purple pansies and yellow daisies forming a border. She bought a new queen-sized bed with a pink comforter. She bought herself a large pink vanity and covered its surface with dozens of bottles of lotions and perfumes and conditioners.

Arvo was amazed by the transformation. Still, Tiltu hated the farm. She told Arvo that she would never like the place no matter how much she changed it. She especially hated living at the end of a trail through the woods. She especially hated the place in the winter when she had to don skis or snowshoes and hike through drifts of snow to get to her car at the turn-around. She particularly hated the abandoned hulks of junker cars all over the property. Without informing Arvo, she called a junk dealer, who came out with heavy equipment and hauled off most of the abandoned vehicles.

Tiltu knew of Arvo's love for the vintage Lincoln, however, and told the junkman to leave it alone. The Lincoln had, by then, sat for several years in the turnaround. Its tires had gone flat, and rust dots had begun to appear all over its body.

Whenever Tiltu told Arvo that she didn't want to live at the farm, he informed her that neither his mother nor his grandmother had liked living there either. "But they got used to it," he said.

"The place killed your grandmother," Tiltu replied, having already heard as much of Arvo's family history as he knew, "and your mother ran into town a dozen times a day. You won't make me a prisoner out here."

Eight months into their marriage, Arvo and Tiltu's son was born. Tiltu liked the idea of being a mother but hated the reality of it. She was overly conscientious about feeding the baby, keeping him clean in cute clothes and keeping the entire house neat and orderly. Then, when her second child, a daughter, arrived a year and a half later, she could no longer take the strictures imposed by motherhood. At first she merely demanded that they get a babysitter and go out every weekend, but when they went out to restaurants, Arvo usually wanted a place that served great chucks of meat, and she wanted ambiance and pasta. They tried going to dances, but he wanted to listen to a band playing classic country and western, and she wanted to dance to hard rock.

Soon she began to demand that he return home immediately after his last class. "But I often have tests to run off, students to meet, or other duties that I didn't get to during the day," he argued.

"I don't care!" she would reply. "I'm stuck with these kids all day while you're off doing what you like to do. I need to get out of here for a little while."

So, Arvo rushed out of school every afternoon and returned home. Frequently Tiltu left him with the little ones while she fled into the night, usually implying that she was going to visit girlfriends, but often she went directly to a bar to drink for three or four hours.

Once, in the third year of their marriage, when Tiltu was supposed to be doing volunteer work at the community center, Arvo found her car parked in front of the home of one of Tiltu's old boyfriends. Arvo parked, left the children in the car and approached the building. He tried the back and front doors, but both were locked. Arvo pounded on each door for a long time, and then gave each a few sold kicks, but no one replied. Arvo drove the children home. Moments later, Tiltu was there, too, with a story about stopping at the boyfriend's to smoke some dope. "I didn't have sex with him!" she insisted.

Arvo didn't believe her, especially after he spotted her car at the ex-boyfriend's house a second time, when she was supposed to be visiting a girl-friend in Twin Lakes. After that, Arvo never fully trusted Tiltu again, and yet she usually got her way because he hated her tantrums. She formed a habit of leaving Arvo with the children while they showered and got ready for bed. She knew he couldn't hunt for her once the children were in bed, and she always had a good story about where she had been. Sometimes, though, she got violently angry over nothing and stormed off to the bars for hours. Once she came home several hours after the bars had closed. "I went for a ride with one of the Heikkinen boys," she said. "But we didn't have sex. He wanted to, but I wouldn't let him."

Other times she called from the bars and said hateful and cruel things to Arvo. After she hung up, he would go upstairs to look at his sleep-ing son and daughter. "Don't be like your mother when you grow up," he would whisper to them.

Once Tiltu stayed out all night and said she'd slept alone in a motel room near the casino in Baraga.

Somehow the marriage lasted ten years. Arvo felt that those years had been like a roller-coaster ride—sometimes full of elation, but always full of fear. He loved Tiltu more than he ought. He knew that. She was intelligent, neat, well groomed and beautiful. She took good care of the children when she wasn't in one of her moods. She seemed to love them. Sometimes she even seemed to love him, though she had an odd definition of spousal love. She cooked delicious meals, made pies for holidays and made raspberry, thimbleberry and blueberry jams at the end of each summer. She kept the house orderly and very clean, and she had the sense of interior decoration of a professional. The farmhouse walls hosted beautiful arrangements of pictures, artificial flowers, and tin birds. There were a lot of shelves with knickknacks and scented candles. Tiltu still laughed a lot, enjoyed a good joke and socialized with her own and Arvo's friends. Recently, she had begun to diet in combination with long workouts and walks and had lost fifteen pounds. She was wonderful in bed. She had wonderful taste concerning clothes and make-up. She gardened. She had the ability to talk to anyone from the lowest sort of barfly to educated people such as the teachers at Jeffers.

In the eleventh year of their marriage, Tiltu discovered the pleasures of gambling. Her gambling began harmlessly enough when she met Kristi Herrala, and they became good friends. Kristi was older than Tiltu, twice divorced and liked to spend her Saturday evenings playing Bingo in the basement of the Lutheran Church. One Saturday, Tiltu went with her new friend, but Tiltu quickly became dissatisfied with the prizes. Many were potholders made from squares of flannel sewn together by members of the Martha and Mary Society. Kristi herself was a member of the society, and, over the years, she had won dozens of potholders, many of them made by herself.

That evening, Tiltu won three potholders, all of them markedly different in design, but none of them matching the colors of Tiltu's kitchen. When Tiltu voiced her dissatisfaction, Kristi told her about the new Bingo hall beside the casino on the Keweenaw Indian Reservation in Baraga. "All the prizes are in cash, and you can win hundreds of dollars," Kristi told her. So, the following Saturday night, Tiltu and Kristi drove the forty miles to Baraga in Kristi's new Camry.

Within a month, Tiltu discovered the slot machines in the nearby casino. Soon she was driving alone to Baraga to play the slots every

Wednesday and Saturday and sometimes a night or two in between. For a short time, she played the nickel machines, but soon she graduated to quarters. Not long after that, she discovered the dollar and five-dollar machines.

She also discovered the cheap drinks at the bar. The drinks made her reckless, and she didn't mind losing one hundred dollars in ten minutes as long as she had the possibility of striking it rich one night. *It only takes the right combination one time, and I'll be set for life*, she told herself.

At first, Tiltu kissed Arvo goodbye after supper, promised to show him a good time when she returned and drove off to Baraga for several hours. She usually returned by ten.

But, within a month, she was staying until one or two in the morning. When she returned, she reeked of smoke and alcohol and was too tired to show Arvo anything. Often she had a headache.

Arvo had never been in a casino and assumed it was something like the Bingo at the Lutheran Church but on a bigger scale. *They probably won nickels instead of potholders*, he thought. When the next checking account statement arrived, Arvo discovered that he was penniless at the bank. In a fever, he called a second bank, where he and Tiltu kept their savings. The amount had been halved. Arvo was horrified. Tiltu had driven to the mall to shop for household necessities, and then was going over to Kristi's for coffee and *nisu*. She wouldn't be back for two or three hours.

Arvo loaded the kids into his truck and drove frantically to the mall, but Tiltu wasn't there. Then he drove to Kristi's, but she wasn't there either. He returned home and waited. When Tiltu finally returned around seven that evening, she was drunk.

"Where have you been?" he asked her.

"Kristi and I went out for a drink," Tiltu told him.

"Kristi hasn't seen you for days. I just talked to her," Arvo told her. "Where have you really been?"

Tiltu told him she had been at the casino.

Arvo waved the bank statement in front of her eyes. "You've been losing an average of three hundred and sixty dollars every time you visit that place," he said and waited for her to own up and beg his forgiveness.

Instead, she grew haughty. She glared at him as if he were an annoying insect. "We need to talk," she said.

"We certainly do," said Arvo.

"I've met someone," said Tiltu.

"What are you talking about?" asked Arvo, shocked by this sudden turn of events.

"I was playing the slots about a month ago, and I could feel someone looking at me. I turned around, and there he was. It was almost as if he had undressed me from across the room. His eyes caressed me everywhere. Then he walked over and asked if I wanted to take a ride."

"What are you talking about?" said Arvo again.

"So, we did. We drove down by the water and talked."

"Just talked?" asked Arvo.

"That time, we just talked. Since then, we've met several times. We've only had sex a couple of times. It didn't mean anything. I love you, not him."

"Do you want a divorce? Is that what this is all about?" Arvo asked.

"No," said Tiltu. "I told you the truth. It didn't mean anything to me. I was drunk every time I went with him. It was just something to do."

"Like munching an apple is just something to do?"

"You're angry. Don't get mad," said Tiltu. "It was nothing."

"Who is this guy?" asked Arvo.

"You don't need to know," said Tiltu.

"Yes, I do," said Arvo. "I'd like to kill the son of a bitch."

"But, he didn't do anything," said Tiltu. "It was me."

"Who is he?" asked Arvo.

"His name is Dub Santti. He's a logger."

"I know who he is," said Arvo. "Don't forget—my father was a logger. Loggers know each other. Santti. You've got to be kidding. He's from a strange family. His mother believes in witchcraft, and his kid is out of control and weird. Dub himself is simple—dumb really. His brain must be the size of an acorn."

"It's not the size of his brain that I was interested in," said Tiltu. "I can't talk anymore about this right now. I have to get cleaned up first."

"You're drunk right now," said Arvo. "I can smell the alcohol from across the room, and you're slurring your words."

"I need a shower," said Tiltu, and she disappeared toward the bathroom.

Arvo walked into the kitchen, took a cup from the cupboard and poured himself a cup of coffee from the electric coffee maker on the counter. The coffee tasted flat and sour. *These things should never have replaced the old-fashioned percolators,* Arvo thought. He sat down at the kitchen table and noticed the unopened mail that lay where he'd tossed it after he'd opened the bank statements and discovered that Tiltu had lost tens of thousands of dollars in the casino. One of the unopened pieces was the phone bill. Arvo ripped it open. The bill was for a little more than three hundred dollars. Attached were three pages of long distance calls to a number in Watton. *It's got to be Dub Santti's number,* Arvo realized. *The son of a bitch has been having phone sex with my wife four or fives times every day, and I'm supposed to pay for it.* Arvo felt like he was going to explode. He read the list of calls from top to bottom, from page one to the last page. Some of the calls had lasted over an hour.

The world turned white hot around Arvo. He seemed to walk through flames to the bathroom door. Inside, he could hear water spattering over his wife's body. He thought of Judas trying to wash his hands. *She'll never get the filth off!* he thought. *And her soul will still be dirty no matter how long she soaks herself.* He opened the door a crack. Tiltu was a shadow behind the shower curtain. She was singing an old Bee Gee's song. She seemed unconcerned about anything. *The bitch is actually happy,* Arvo thought. He wanted to wring his wife's neck, to throttle her. He liked the word "throttle." It sounded deadly.

"I just opened the phone bill," he told her with a shaky voice.

"You're letting cold air in," she shouted over the curtain.

"You can pay for all those calls to Watton!" he shouted above the spray of the water.

Tiltu kept right on showering. She began to shampoo her hair with the very expensive shampoo she bought from a cosmetologist in Houghton. "Don't get hysterical!" she told Arvo.

"It's three hundred dollars, and I'm not paying it!" shouted Arvo. "And we're getting separate accounts."

"You're being ridiculous," replied Tiltu. "We can't have separate accounts. I don't even work. Is that all you're concerned about? The money?"

"Of course not!" shouted Arvo. He found it impossible to control his anger, and his voice rose to a screech. "I want to know why you've been screwing around with another guy—especially somebody as dumb as Santti. He didn't even finish high school. Have you no respect for me or your marriage vows?"

"You're yelling. I'm not going to talk to you when you're upset. Now, leave me alone so that I can finish rinsing my hair. And shut the door when you leave. I don't want to freeze when I get out to dry off." Tiltu turned her back to him and became again a mute outline behind the shower curtain. Water spayed noisily through her hair.

Arvo retreated to the kitchen, sat down and poured himself a fresh cup of the flat coffee. He wanted to calm his nerves with good coffee from the percolator that Tiltu had thrown out of the house years ago, during the period when she had renovated everything in his life. He stared straight ahead at the kitchen wall and wondered what to do. His world seemed to be collapsing around him. And yet, Tiltu was irritatingly calm. *She ought to be coming to me on her knees, begging forgiveness,* he thought.

Arvo's daughter was in the living room, drawing. She sometimes spent hours inventing wardrobes for princesses and drawing and coloring these on sheets of white paper. Arvo heard the front door open and close and knew without looking that his son had come in from outside. The son often spent hours in the woods, building forts and tree houses and fighting imaginary wars against space aliens. The boy would never be able to live off the land, but he could transform it into a place as fantastic as the cartoons he watched on TV. Soon Arvo heard scuffling. "Dad!" his daughter screamed. "He's got my picture and won't give it back! Dad, he's rippin' my picture!"

Arvo rose from his chair, walked to the doorway and glared at his son, but the boy sat quietly on the couch, watching TV as if he hadn't moved in hours. His daughter sat cross-legged on the floor with a pile of drawings in front of her and scattered about the room. She also glared at the boy.

Arvo retreated again to the kitchen and his coffee. He heard Tiltu coming from the bathroom and prepared himself for another confrontation. Tiltu entered the kitchen on a tilt. She wore her bathrobe and had a great towel wrapped around her wet hair. Her face was beet red from the hot water and the alcohol. Her hands clung to the sides of the doorway for support. Her eyes blazed with a fierce energy, the pupils large and deep. She was clearly very drunk—much more so than she had been thirty minutes earlier when she had arrived home. Arvo knew that whenever she got that drunk, she became loud, belligerent and verbally abusive. Sometimes she threw things. Arvo remembered a long list of items she had destroyed. In a fury, she began to shout, repeating herself again and again—the same sentences, the same thoughts, mixed with spittle, flying across the room. "You were sitting right there when your son tore Susan's paper," Tiltu shouted. "Why didn't you stop him? I was in the bathroom, and I could hear what was going on. Why didn't you react?"

Arvo admitted that he should have gotten up from the table sooner and gone in. "I should have stopped their arguing before the paper got ripped," he said.

"You were sitting right there when Billy tore the picture," Tiltu said for what seemed to be the fiftieth time. "Why didn't you stop it? I was in the bathroom, and I could hear everything. They didn't stop until I yelled from the bathroom."

"Actually, Billy had moved away from Susan, and it was over in a couple of seconds," said Arvo. "And I didn't hear you yell."

"You were sitting right there when Billy tore Susan's paper," said Tiltu.

"You're drunk, and repeating yourself," Arvo said.

"So, now it's my fault," exclaimed Tiltu. "Because I drink too much. It's never your fault, of course. You never admit that you're wrong."

"No one said it was anybody's fault," said Arvo. "And I already admitted that I should have intervened faster."

"No, it's never your fault," Tiltu said again. "You always blame me. It's my drinking."

"No one said it was your fault," Arvo said again.

"Oh, yes you did," said Tiltu. "All the problems between us are always Tiltu's fault. Never Arvo's. Why didn't you stop your kids from fighting? You were sitting right there. You're a coward. You're only half a man. You're weak."

"There must be something wrong with me," admitted Arvo, "because you've been driving to Baraga every chance you get in order to lose three or four thousand dollars on the slots and in order to have sex with your boyfriend from Watton."

"I was in the bathroom drying my hair, and I kept thinking, 'Why doesn't he say something?' That's why I go to the casino and to Watton. I want a real man, not a wimp."

"You're drunk," said Arvo.

"You've had just as much to drink today as I have," said Tiltu.

"Yes, but I drank coffee," Arvo pointed out.

"Well, it's over now," cried Tiltu. "I've already gotten a lawyer—a good one. Someone has given me thousands of dollars for the best. I'm going to take you for every penny you've got. I'll be a rich woman after I get rid of you."

"Your boyfriend? Is he your wealthy benefactor?" asked Arvo accusingly. "I pity the man. I suppose you'll screw him over someday just like you've been destroying me for the last months."

Tiltu stormed across the kitchen and yanked the phone off its stand on the wall. She stormed back to the table and thrust the phone at Arvo, its cord taut. "Here!" she shouted. "Call a lawyer. It's over."

"Don't be ridiculous," Arvo said. "It's almost eight P.M. I couldn't call even if I wanted to. And I don't want to."

"Can't you get it through your thick Finnish head? We're through," cried Tiltu. "I've got three people who will give me the money to support myself. Call a lawyer."

"Put the phone away!" said Arvo, trying to reason with her but knowing it was hopeless. "You're very drunk," he said again.

"Sure, blame it on my drinking!" cried Tiltu. "You're such a saint! You never do anything wrong!"

"I'm not the one having an affair," replied Arvo. "Why did you have to pick up Dub Santti? The guy is kind of a joke. Other loggers used to tease him about all the venereal diseases he picked up in Vietnam. He may have given you one. You may have passed it on to me."

"Call a lawyer!" cried Tiltu, and she thrust the phone again and again into Arvo's face.

Arvo took the phone, rose from the table and walked across the room to put it back on its rest, but Tiltu saw what he was doing and once again grabbed the phone while he was still holding it. They began to wrestle for control of the phone. Tiltu, acting like a crazy woman, gasped for air and pushed and pulled and shoved and scratched, but Arvo held on. Several times one or the other lost balance. They caromed from the table to the refrigerator to the sink. Then Tiltu bit down as hard as she could on Arvo's finger.

"Stop it!" he cried in pain, but she kept right on biting. *My God! She's going right down to the bone!* Arvo realized, so he slapped her face as hard as he could.

She stopped biting and leaned her head back, her wild eyes staring into his. "That's it!" she cried in strange exultation. "Now I can call the cops. You just lost the kids, the farm, everything! You just made my day!" and she spit in his face.

Still, they wrestled over the phone. Then Arvo noticed that the children stood in the doorway, watching. Both were terribly upset and crying. "Put on your coats and go to a neighbor's," Arvo told them. "Take a flashlight. When you get there, tell them to call the sheriff. Tell them your mother has gone crazy."

"I'm afraid," said Susan. "I don't know what to do!"

"Go to the neighbor's." Arvo tried to sound firm but calm.

Susan didn't move. Billy ran upstairs. Tiltu leaned her head back and began to scream. She reminded Arvo of a she-wolf. Tiltu's wail went on and on, filling the house. Susan put her hands over her ears. Arvo let go of the phone to go to his daughter. Tiltu immediately ran across the kitchen, ripped the cord out of the wall and ran outside. When Arvo went to the window, Tiltu was not in sight. She had disappeared down the path that led to the turnaround.

In the sudden quiet, Arvo set out to calm his children. He made them butterscotch pudding as a treat and sat with them in the living room while they ate it. Not much later, a policeman came through the door and arrested Arvo for assault and battery.

Arvo was handcuffed and led off to the squad car at the turnaround. He was put into the back seat while a second officer sat in the front. The first officer then went over to another squad car where Tiltu sat. The officer took pictures of Tiltu's face and then brought out a tape recorder and took a long and rambling and often incoherent statement from her.

"What about the kids?" Arvo asked the cop.

"They'll be taken care of," said the cop. They sat in silence for what seemed a long time. Arvo remembered how much his father and grandfather had hated cops, courts, and lawyers. He began to understand why.

"Once the process starts, it's automatic," the cop said. "In domestic violence cases, the guy is given twenty-four hours in jail. It's a calming down period. In the morning there'll be a hearing, and you can post bail. Then you'll be released. You won't be able to go home though. There will be a thirty-day restraining order against you. You won't be able to go near your wife or kids unless she agrees that you can see the kids through a third party. If you're seen talking to her, you'll be arrested again."

Arvo didn't say anything.

"We know about your wife's affair," said the cop. "She was parked somewhere in Baraga County late last night with her boyfriend. An officer down there checked them out. A person can't do anything around here without everyone else knowing about it. Plus, her boyfriend has been in court before. He's divorced."

Arvo had always philosophically supported domestic violence laws, but he never thought he would be subject to them.

"You should've thrown all her stuff out while she was somewhere else and then locked the door," the cop added. "She got you as soon as you hit her."

The back of the squad car did not give much leg room. Arvo was forced to twist himself to the side to relieve the pressure. Still, his knees ached.

At the county jail, a young cop fingerprinted Arvo and took his mug shot. Then he removed Arvo's belt, watch, shoe laces, and wedding ring and dug into his pockets. He stared for a long time at Arvo's over-large pen knife and the sheathed hunting knife. Arvo wanted to tell the kid that these weren't signs of criminality, but he said nothing. The young cop asked Arvo a lot of questions—his mother's maiden name, his birth date, whether or not he felt suicidal sometimes. "Who hasn't?" said Arvo. The cop marked "yes" by that question.

All the deputies were very polite to Arvo in an indifferent kind of way. One of them had been a student of Arvo's years before. He came over to shake Arvo's hand and asked him if he wanted to make a statement. So, Arvo told the cop what had happened. "You should have left her the first time she drove down to Baraga without you," the cop advised.

Soon Arvo was ensconced in his cell. The stainless steel toilet was without a seat and didn't flush properly. The toilet roll contained only a couple of sheets of paper. A cup was styrofoam. The cot was gray metal with sharp lines and hard angles. The mattress and pillow were vinyl and gave no support to tired bones. The cinder block walls were white.

The former student brought Arvo the rolling jail bookcase and left it in the hall. Arvo could reach through the bars to select a book if he wished. Most of the books had been donated as a tax write-off by an organization of university professors. Arvo, along with the local drunks, petty thieves and vagrants, could select works by Malcolm Lowry, Herman Hesse, Simone de Beauvoir, Jean Paul Sartre, Thomas Mann, and Graham Greene. Tucked in among these classics were simplified readers about Jesus and alcoholism. Arvo selected a tome by Dostoevsky and, because the bed was infernally hard, stood by the bars for the remainder of the night and tried to read by the glow of a forty-watt bulb that hung from the ceiling down the hallway.

In the morning, the rolling breakfast cart brought Arvo three pancakes and a dab of syrup on a melmac plate. The spoonful of orange juice was in a three-ounce Dixie cup. "What are you in here for?" asked the breakfast carter, who looked like he had just come from a maximum-security prison himself.

"I married the wrong woman," Arvo replied.

"Domestic," said the breakfast guy as he rolled his cart down the hall and out of sight.

The gray-barred door of Arvo's cell looked out onto the fire-engine-red maximum-security cell door. That door was layers of steel welded together and studded with rivets. Its tiny window of unbreakable glass was cracked from the inside.

The breakfast-cart guy came by again, but he carried a broom, plunger, Pinesol, a mop, a bucket, and a roll of paper towels. "Do you want to clean your room?" he asked Arvo. "It's a daily thing. If you think it's dirty, you're given the opportunity to scrub it down."

Arvo didn't say anything.

The man left.

Somewhere a radio endlessly played current pop music.

A guard named Jack opened up the maximum-security door and let a tall orange-clad palsied inmate walk with him down the hall to some unspecified destination. The inmate wore shackles and handcuffs. In a few minutes, they were back, the inmate entered his cell, and the door slammed shut with a loud clanking of metal against metal.

An hour later, Arvo was led from his cell to the nearby courthouse for his hearing. The entire process only lasted a few minutes. The judge asked him how he would plead, and Arvo said nothing, so the judge decided he was pleading not guilty. "Get a lawyer," he told Arvo.

A sour-faced overweight woman in the back of the courtroom said that she was from the shelter and that she represented the poor abused victim. She asked the judge to instate a thirty-day restraining order against Arvo with an automatic extension if the victim desired it. The judge complied and set bail.

Arvo returned to his cell but shortly afterwards was led to the sheriff's office. The sheriff offered Arvo a cup of coffee and a doughnut. Clearly he was trying to be friendly, but Arvo had been taught all his life to be distrustful of anyone representing government and law. "You're a teacher," the sheriff said.

Arvo nodded.

"Do you have cash with you for the bail?" the sheriff asked.

Arvo explained that he only had his check book and some change.

"A check won't do," said the sheriff. "She's probably already cleaned out the account. Probably all of your accounts if they're joint. Do you have someone you could call who would make bail for you?"

Arvo couldn't think of anyone. He didn't want to call one of the teachers from his school. Plus, he didn't consider any of them to be a close friend. Except for Tiltu, he'd been a loner for many years.

"Maybe you should call a lawyer," recommended the sheriff. "There's a bevy of them right across the street."

Arvo explained that he hated lawyers.

"We all do," said the sheriff with sympathy, "but sometimes they're necessary."

Arvo asked what they cost.

"Usually around one hundred and twenty dollars an hour," the sheriff said.

Arvo was shocked.

"Of course, you'll have to give him a retainer fee," the sheriff explained.

Arvo again wanted to know how much that would be.

"Most want around three thousand dollars," the sheriff said.

Arvo looked apoplectic. After several sips of coffee, he asked the sheriff what would happen if he called a lawyer right then.

"None may take you on as a client because they don't yet have the retainer," the sheriff explained. "Plus, they'll charge you for the call. If one of them is willing to pay your bail, he'll probably also charge you for writing out the check and bringing it over here. It might be an extra hundred bucks or so. If you get out, do you have a place to go? Will a friend put you up for the next couple of months?"

Arvo's future sounded pretty complicated and denigrating. The most they could give him for slapping Tiltu's face was ninety-three days in jail. The room and board was cheap, and the company was bearable. Arvo decided to stay. "To hell with judges, lawyers, and abusive women," said Arvo. He finished his coffee, and a deputy led him back to his cell.

In the middle of Arvo's ninety-three-day sentence, he received his one and only phone call, from a downstate wildlife biologist in East Lansing. He and his wife were setting up an environmental station in the middle of the woods about a half mile from the dead-end turnaround of Salonen Avenue. To get to the station, visitors would have to follow a path that crossed Arvo's property. The biologist wanted permission. Arvo gave it.

"I'd also like permission to move an ancient, rusting car that sits at the turnaround," said the biologist. "We intend to bring bus loads of school children out to the station, and in the winter the buses won't have room to turn around with that car in the way."

Arvo explained that he was very fond of the car and didn't want it moved, especially when he wasn't there to decide where it should be put.

When Arvo finally went home, the notification of the divorce action was in the mailbox, along with a huge pile of bills and irate and threatening letters from credit agencies. Arvo had already been to the banks. Tiltu had disappeared with every penny. During his incarceration, winter had arrived, and the pipes in the unheated farmhouse had burst, flooding the floors with a thin layer of ice. The divorce decree stated that, until everything was divided, he was not allowed to stay at the farmhouse, but he moved in anyway. He learned from Kristi that Tiltu and the children were in Green Bay—that Tiltu was an exotic dancer in a downtown club. She had a small apartment, a new boyfriend who made a good living as a blackjack dealer in a casino. While Arvo was sitting in jail, he had been fired as a teacher.

All of this infuriated him. Plus, his 1940s twelve-cylinder Lincoln was gone. Just back from jail, he followed the path out to the Environmental Station to find out the fate of his car. It had been impounded by the county. "We had to get it out of the way," explained the wildlife biologist. "The school buses couldn't turn around."

Arvo returned to the Sheriff's Department at the jailhouse and explained his problem. The sheriff dug through his files and pulled out the report on the Lincoln. "You're talking about that rusting heap from out in Misery Bay? We've got it," said the sheriff. "I think Jack handled it. He's just down the hall. I'll call him. He'll be here in a minute."

When Jack appeared, he verified that the case of the Lincoln had been his. "The Environmental Station made a complaint. You want it back?"

Arvo said that he did.

"You'll have to pay for the impoundment and the towing, both ways," explained Jack. "Plus, it's an endangerment to the school kids going out to the Environmental Station. It was on the highway but not insured. It has no pollution control on the exhaust system. One window was cracked, the brakes are frozen with rust. I've got a long list of everything that's wrong with the car. All of it will have to be fixed at your expense before we can let you have it. It's going to cost you a couple of thousand dollars. You can't just leave a heap like that on a public road."

"It's not on a public road," said Arvo. "All of that road is on my property. My grandfather built it. I can show you the deed."

"But the county plows it," argued Jack.

"Out of courtesy," said Arvo. "No one in my family ever asked them to. They can stop tomorrow, for all I care."

"But that road leads to the Environmental Station," said Jack.

"No, it doesn't. The station is a half mile to the southeast. They park buses on my road, and they use a path that crosses my property. On my property, I can park a car in any kind of condition. I can use it for target practice if that pleases me."

Jack owned property himself and had, years before, tried to get permission from the DNR to drain a swampy tract in one corner. He had been told that the swamp was a natural wetland, and permission had been denied. "I see your point," he told Arvo. "Why don't you speak to the people at the station?"

For years Arvo had had NO HUNTING and NO TRESPASSING signs scattered around his property. Some were really old and went back to his father's time. The ones that said PÄÄSY KIELLETTY were put up by his grandfather. Arvo collected half a dozen, including one in Finnish and nailed them to trees by the entrance of the path to the Environmental Station.

It wasn't long before the wildlife biologist was at Arvo's door. "The path is mine. The road is mine," Arvo told him.

"How are we going to get school children to the station?" the biologist asked.

"Build your own damned road," said Arvo.

A few days later, the Lincoln was back in its former exact spot at the turnaround. The wildlife biologist had used some of the Environmental Station's state funding to pay for its return, its impoundment, and the original towing charges. The biologist had spent over an hour talking the sheriff into dropping all fines and repairs that Jack had listed in his original report. "Hell," said the sheriff finally. "I might as well just throw this report away," and he rolled it into a ball and tossed it into his wastebasket.

After measuring with his eye the car's location and after inspecting the Lincoln to ensure that its condition had been neither improved nor worsened, Arvo took down all the NO TRESPASSING signs.

Arvo went to work in the woods. Using his property as collateral, he borrowed three thousand dollars from Northland Savings and Loan and retained a lawyer so he could get his kids back. The lawyer kept the money for a while, spent $2,400 on a half dozen phone calls and four or five letters, and then informed Arvo that he didn't have a chance in hell of ever getting his kids back. "In the eyes of the law, she's a saint and you're a devil," said the lawyer. "Plus, she's gone out of state. That makes the process almost impossible."

Eventually, the divorce came through. Tiltu got the money and the kids. Arvo got the farm and mid-week visitation whenever he could get down to Green Bay, four and one-half hours away, which wasn't often. Tiltu had insisted on a Wednesday/Thursday visitation so that she could rest up for Friday and Saturday nights, when she made most of her income by dancing naked or nearly naked in front of drunk Packers fans, college kids, casino prowlers, and miscreants of every kind. Arvo was happy to be rid of her. He vowed never to have anything to do with a woman again.

Years passed. Arvo grew old and even more eccentric. He spent part of every day in the Lincoln, taking dream drives to Helsinki, Tahiti, and Butte, Montana. On a late fall afternoon, he sat behind the wheel of the old car when a bus load of fourth graders arrived from Hancock Elementary School. They were on a field trip with their teacher to see the birds at the Environmental Station. While Arvo imagined a drive to Ashtabula, Ohio, the fourth graders snickered at him and pointed. Arvo didn't see them. He was approaching Ashtabula, looking for Finns.

One day Arvo decided to fulfill his dreams. By then he again had a little money in the bank, and his kids had grown. Arvo packed up his old pickup and drove off into America to document the Finnish diaspora. For three days, he drove east, mostly inside Canada, in order to visit first the little slate-mining community of Monson, way up in the wilds of north-central Maine, near Moosehead Lake. He stayed in a boarding house with a clientele of Appalachian Trail hikers, and he took photos of the eighteen open pits scattered around the town. He visited a museum of local history, the library, and the Finnish Farmers' Hall, where they still held Finnish dances once a month. Arvo interviewed Jorma Ranta, an old man who had played polkas and *radikkas* at the hall for more than fifty years.

From Monson, Arvo drove to South Paris, Maine, and then on to Fitchburg, Massachusetts. He visited a Finnish community in Brooklyn and upper New York State. He drove way down to Lake Worth, Florida, and in north to Fairport Harbor, Warren, and Ashtabula, Ohio. He went home for a while, then took a trip west into Minnesota, the Dakotas, Montana, the Northwest, and Arizona.

After months on the road, he returned to his home and sat down in the farmhouse's kitchen to write. With a number-two pencil, he set out to write the definitive history of Finns in the United States. He was tired but worked on through the gray light, flurries, blizzards, and extreme cold of what his grandfather had called the ox-weeks of late December, January, and the first half of February. Then he reached the weeks of hope, *Toivon Viikot*, when the sun came out again but with little warmth, the world still white and frosty.

Arvo worked for two years to get the book into its final manuscript form. Then he found out that no one would publish it. "Who would buy it?" publishers asked. Eventually, Arvo self-published it at considerable cost. A few Copper Country bookstores and gift shops agreed to try to sell copies on a commission basis, with all unsold copies reverting to Arvo. In the first year, Arvo tried to revitalize sales by sending out review copies to newspapers but only one, the Finnish-language Communist paper in Superior, Wisconsin, chose to review it, and that paper only talked about the single chapter on Finnish socialists. In Finnish. Arvo didn't know written Finnish and couldn't read the only review his book got.

Undeterred, Arvo decided to write another book, this one about Canadian Finns. *Maybe Canadians will be more appreciative*, he thought. On a January Friday when a blizzard had made working in the woods impossible, Arvo packed up the pickup and headed through whiteouts for Sudbury in northern Ontario. He looked forward to more research and to seeing the giant nickel perched on a tailing heap. At the border post in Sault St. Marie, a Canadian customs official asked Arvo for his name and the nature of his business in Canada. Arvo gave his name and explained that he was a writer doing research on Finns.

Immediately, several more customs officials and a mountie ordered Arvo to pull his vehicle off to the side of the road and get out. Arvo was detained at the border for two hours and ultimately was not allowed in Canada. Arvo wanted to know why.

"Your name is on a list," explained the customs official.

Arvo wanted to know what kind of a list.

"We keep a list of *persona non grata*," explained the official. "Most are on the list for criminality or terrorism, a few for politics. You're on there for political reasons. The FBI presumably forwarded your name to Ottawa, and we've been ordered to keep you out of Canada because you're dangerous."

"But I'm just a logger from northern Michigan," said Arvo. "And I've only written one book, which nobody read."

"The books nobody reads are the very ones that usually get somebody's name on the list," explained the customs man. "What kind of a book is it?"

"It's a history of Finns in North America," said Arvo.

"I'll bet you've got a chapter about Finnish union organizers working for the IWW in the copper mines of Michigan and on the iron range of Minnesota," said the customs official. "I'll bet that you even had a relative, a grandfather or somebody else, who was a socialist back in 1914 or in the twenties or thirties."

"That's right," said Arvo. "How did you know? In fact, I've got lots of unsold copies right here in my truck bed inside some boxes."

The customs official wanted to see the books, so Arvo walked to the back of the truck and pointed out the boxes. He had covered them with a tarp to keep them dry.

The customs official immediately ordered the seizure and impound-ment of all copies. He explained to Arvo that he had to do it because they were subversive. He apologized to Arvo as he and two other uniformed men carried the boxes away. "I actually hate to take them, but it's the law," he told Arvo. The official was half-Finnish and from Thunder Bay, Ontario, a largely Finnish community at the western end of Lake Superior. He, too, he said, had had a Communist grandfather. "But I'm not dumb enough to advertise it in a book," he said.

The customs official invited Arvo inside his office and brought him a cup of coffee and a smoked Lake Superior chub. "You know, Arvo, you're in good company," explained the official while Arvo ate and drank. "One of our greatest Canadian writers, Farley Mowat, is not allowed in the States for the same reason you're not allowed into Canada. Farley wrote *Never Cry Wolf*. It was made into a movie, but he wasn't allowed to be at its premiere in California because he also wrote a book called *The Siberians*, about nomadic Arctic people of Russia."

Suddenly Arvo felt very proud. He and Farley Mowat and people like Fidel Castro were now in the same crowd—on the same list.

When he finished the chub and coffee, Arvo said goodbye and got back in the pickup to drive the four and one-half hours back to Misery Bay. As he drove, he felt good. He felt like somebody. He felt like an outlaw, like a Finnish version of Butch Cassidy or the Sundance Kid. He suddenly remembered with fondness his time in the slammer . . . the Big House . . . the Pen. He felt as one with his grandfather and with a long line of Finnish radicals—Communists, anarchists, founders of co-operatives, temperance members, and union advocates. All he needed now was a thick venison steak fried with onions and washed down with several cups of strong percolator-brewed coffee and his day would be complete.

Tapiola

Chapter Seven

Väinämöinen

From time immemorial Väinämöinen had wandered the forests and lakeshores of Finland, creating order and beauty with his kantele, his magical harp. When he grew angry, he sang his enemies into swamps, and when happiness moved him, the sun and moon stopped to listen and the lakes smoothed to glass. Väinämöinen's kantele was made from the jawbone of a giant pike. Its strings were as mysterious as spider webs and frozen dew. Väinämöinen plucked those strings with fingers that could be as powerful as eagle claws or as soft as mink fur.

By 1987, Väinämöinen had grown bitter. People irritated him. It seemed to him that ever since the creation, people had done the same stupid things in the same stupid ways. His hope wavered and he often found himself sick in the soul. He needed change. Then he heard stories of a remarkable kantele player on the other side of the world, in a place with a strange name: the Upper Peninsula of Michigan. The kantele player, called an American, had studied music at the Sibelius Academy in Helsinki, and that impressed Väinämöinen. After all, Sibelius had been a pretty good musician in his day. For a while, Sibelius was Väinämöinen's stiffest competition, but, in the end, Väinämöinen was certain that he himself had prevailed. Sibelius had grown cranky in his old age. Maybe that happened to all musicians, thought Väinämöinen. He felt it, too, at times. And now an upstart American, from so far away it might as well be the end of the Earth, was building a reputation as a great kantele player. The man had even recorded.

Väinämöinen's arthritic knee ached, and an odd twinge that ran from his elbow to the fingertips of his right hand had recurred. These uncomfortable pains certainly didn't improve his cranky humor. In a black mood, Väinämöinen threw a few clothes into an ancient backpack, tossed his cell phone on top of the clothes, tied the pack shut and slipped one of its straps over his right shoulder. He tucked his kantele under his powerful right arm and flew off to an obscure place called Tapiola, Michigan, to hear this new musician and size up the level of his competition.

On a Sunday afternoon in August, Väinämöinen found himself surrounded by hungry senior citizens in a diner next door to a place called Karvakko's. As far as he could tell, the diner and Karvakko's were the only businesses within many miles. The diner seemed to cater to customers who looked every bit as gnarled and weathered as Väinämöinen himself. He wondered if they, too, had lived a thousand years. Over by the buffet and just behind the salad bar sat an elfin-looking fellow with thinning gray-blonde hair, a round face, and a red complexion. He wore a loose and wrinkled linen shirt not unlike Väinämöinen's. On his lap rested an expensive, factory-made kantele similar to hundreds that Väinämöinen had seen over the centuries. The man was playing a traditional piece that Väinämöinen instantly recognized. The man played beautifully, but Väinämöinen thought that most of the magic was missing. As earthly music, the man created some of the finest that Väinämöinen had heard, but it would never stop the sun in its tracks. It wouldn't even stop the moon.

In the crowded diner Väinämöinen stood out. The pike's jawbone stuck out for several feet from beneath his right arm, and he was wearing a funny, round leather hat without a visor and a laced, rough linen shirt brightly embroidered with blue and yellow flowers. The shirt had not been washed since 1816, but Väinämöinen smelled like spring breezes and was not offensive, at least not to his own most discriminating, thousand-year-old nose.

A busy waitress rushed up to him and asked if he wanted to be seated. Väinämöinen had been standing just inside the entrance for over five minutes, observing the scene and listening to the music. He walked past the waitress and checked out the buffet. Väinämöinen thought the diner certainly believed in supplying quantity. He found a huge mound of mashed potatoes and a deep gravy dish. A patron could choose from among ham, roast beef, and turkey for meats. The vegetables floated in water. The salad bar was mostly lettuce, tomatoes, cucumber, and onion. Väinämöinen declined. He stepped to an empty space of wall and continued to judge the music. Soon the player, whose last name Väinämöinen learned was Kangas, launched into a lively rendition of the "Kurikka Cow Calling Song." Väinämöinen was not impressed. Anyone could call cows. Let him try to call moose or bears.

When the American finished the song, he rose and set his kantele carefully on his chair. He approached the buffet, took a plate and began to select meats and vegetables for his dinner. Väinämöinen watched him silently in disgust. *The man eats like a bird*, he thought. *Little peck here, little peck there.* Väinämöinen himself would have picked thick slabs of all three kinds of meats and probably built a mountain of mashed potatoes on a separate plate.

At the thought of food, Väinämöinen's stomach rumbled. He was hungry. He would have helped himself to the buffet the first time, but he feared that in Michigan in the United States they wouldn't take Finnish marks in payment.

Just then, the American noticed Väinämöinen and greeted him in the peculiar Americanized and old-fashioned Finnish that these people spoke. Väinämöinen, who knew the language of birds and brooks, found variations of Finnish easy. He liked the opportunity to use his Americanized Finnish. The American asked Väinämöinen if he, too, were a player. Väinämöinen replied that he was not just a player. "In Finland, I'm a *pikvila*," he replied with just a little pride.

The American said that he wanted to hear the music of such a big fellow, of such an important person. "Play us a tune," said the American in

English, which Väinämöinen understood as easily as he could understand the language of wolves and mountains and sky.

He nodded and moved over to the musician's chair. He carefully set the man's kantele aside on the floor and then sat down, placed his own kantele, made from the jaw of a huge pike, in his lap and, with a mischievous smile, began to play. From where he sat, Väinämöinen could see out into the diner's kitchen. The cook's helper opened a back door and disappeared outside toward the back of the diner with a bucket of garbage. Concerned that he had not instantly captured everyone's attention, Väinämöinen began to play faster. The back door banged open, and the cook's helper bolted in all out of breath. The back door slammed behind him. "That damned bear is out there again," the cook's helper said to the cook. "He's got his head and front haunches stuck in the trash barrel."

Väinämöinen smiled. After he finished his song, he sat for a short time at the table of the American musician in order to ask if the man was willing to exchange some Finnish marks for American dollars. It turned out that the American was a college music teacher at Suomi College in Hancock. He worked from September through May and had chosen to take all his salary during that time rather than stretch out his biweekly checks through the twelve months. Unfortunately, the American had spent each check as it arrived and, by late summer, had had no money for weeks. "That's why I do these concerts at the diner," the American explained. "I normally play in more impressive concert halls than this, but I need to eat."

Fortunately, the American knew that the old couple at a nearby table was planning a trip to Finland later in the year. They were happy to exchange a few dollars for Väinämöinen's Finnish marks. After stuffing himself with huge mounds of mashed potatoes, well-cooked meats, and watery vegetables, Väinämöinen said goodbye, went outside and headed north toward Lake Superior.

He moved with the speed of an eagle and the stealth of a bobcat, his pack and instrument secure. Soon he spotted a bar called the Mosquito Inn and realized that, though still hungry, he had grown very thirsty. Väinämöinen went inside, chose an empty bar stool and carefully placed his pack and kantele beside him against the base of the bar. When the barmaid approached, Väinämöinen ordered a beer and a Tombstone pizza, extra large. The barmaid wanted to know his choice of beer. Väinämöinen pointed to a large, lit sign behind the bar and said he'd take that kind, so she brought him an Old Milwaukee. The very old guy on the next stool congratulated Väinämöinen on his choice of beer and lifted his own Old Milwaukee in greeting.

From that moment, the two got along famously. The old fart American was named Heikki Heikkinen, and he had been drinking since ten o'clock in the morning. Before that, he'd risen at five and gone fishing on Portage Lake. Apparently, he had caught a number of trout because his shirt front, pants, and hands were smeared with fish offal. He reeked of rotting fish remains, but he didn't seem to mind. He'd worn the same ragged flannel shirt and torn corduroys all week and had been fishing every day. "I don't notice the smell anymore," he said but agreed with Väinämöinen that he probably ought to change clothes soon. "Maybe tomorrow I'll throw them in the wash for the old woman to do," Heikki said as he guzzled down his beer and ordered another with a shot of Kessler's on the side.

Heikki seemed to have an opinion about everything. Retired, he had once been a logger, had worked for a few years for the town of Hancock, owned a boat for summer fishing and a snowmobile for winter fishing and liked to hunt using a pile of bait behind his sauna. The man talked on and on, and Väinämöinen mostly listened. Heikki kept buying new drinks for the two of them, and Väinämöinen never once refused his offer. Väinämöinen eventually got very drunk, and then drunker. To make sure that he didn't do anything incredibly stupid, such as losing his magic kantele, Väinämöinen secured it to his body with his belt and let his pants droop.

Hours passed. Väinämöinen had been on auto pilot for many hours before Heikki finally indicated that it was time to go home. "They close in five minutes," he said.

The two men went outside and climbed into Heikki's pickup. Heikki was too drunk to remember that Väinämöinen was not a member of Heikki's family and, therefore, had no reason to go home with him. Väinämöinen was too drunk even to know that he was in the truck. To keep himself sober enough to drive and awake, Heikki drove with both windows wide open, the cool night air billowing through the cab and whirling about his and Väinämöinen's heads. "This late at night, every damned cop on the road thinks that every driver is drunk," Heikki explained to Väinämöinen, who was falling asleep. "Drunks drink whiskey or vodka or Boone's Farm. We only had beers. We're okay. But try to tell that to a cop."

To fool any officer who might sneak up behind him, Heikki reduced his speed to about eight miles per hour and carefully wove the truck back and forth between the white center line and the bank of the road. That way he'd always be in his own lane.

Some time after three, Heikki steered the pickup into his own driveway, opened his door and fell out of the cab onto the edge of the lawn. Leaving the truck's door open, Heikki crawled toward his front door, entered the house and, still wearing his fish-stained clothes and his greasy swampers, crawled to the couch, climbed onto it, curled up and immediately began to snore loudly.

Some time after four, Väinämöinen woke up in a bent position in the truck cab and wondered where he was and why. He opened the door and staggered out. For a while, he stood on the edge of Heikki's lawn and wondered if he had slipped somehow into hell. A booming rush of pain engulfed his head in waves, and the overhead stars spun wildly. Väinämöinen's shirt was sticky with perspiration, and his long hair stuck up every which way. Väinämöinen eventually noticed a tiny nearby building, obviously used for garden tools, rakes, and shovels. He staggered in that direction, lost his balance halfway there and crawled the remainder of the distance. The door was unlatched and easily swung open. Väinämöinen went inside, curled up on the wooden floor and fell into a deep sleep, his breathing as deep and heavy as a curtain of fog.

Some time after five, Heikki's wife crawled out of bed to start a new day. She planned to work for several hours in the garden and, in particular, to dig up the first of the summer's potatoes—red ones the size of nuggets. She dressed, made coffee in the kitchen, then pulled on a light sweater and her rubber boots to go to work. As she passed the living room, she noticed that her husband had once again passed out on the couch—for the third night in a row. Even from a distance, she could smell him, and his snoring was so loud that she expected the windows to rattle. They didn't, but she showed her disgust for him and his condition by ignoring him and going outside. *Damn him!* she thought as she crossed the yard. *He'll be sleeping for hours! When he wakes he'll be no earthly good to anyone.*

She remembered when he was the love of her life with a twinkle in his lusty blue eyes. Fifty years before, his hair had grown as thick as Iowa corn, and she could lose herself in the golden rush of his chest hair. Now he was as gnarled and twisted as the apple trees in abandoned fields, and he smelled always of booze and smoke and fish and sweat. In his youth, he had worked sixteen-hour days without complaint and could fix virtually anything. He had earned a good living at whatever job he tried, and he had been tender in the dark of their bedroom. Now his soul seemed lightning struck. He had become a kind of human compost heap—ugly and dead on the outside and wormy and dark on the inside. Still, she would stick with him in these last years they had together.

She noticed that the toolshed door hung partway open. As she swung the door open to get a garden spade, she stepped back in fright. It looked like a tramp or vagrant had crawled into their shed and curled up on his side among the rakes and hoes and shovels and died. Then she saw him take a breath and got scared all over that he might be dangerous. The man's right arm hugged something that vaguely resembled a gigantic fish's skeleton.

Väinämöinen awoke at the sound of the door swinging noisily open, but for a moment he was too befogged to react. A steady hammering came from somewhere behind his eyes and dominated his awareness with the pain. He lurched to his feet, steadied himself and stepped out of the shed. Then he saw the woman. She stood perhaps twenty feet away, her eyes watching his every move.

"I can kick like a horse," she said, her voice a bit quavery. "Don't try anything."

"You must be Heikki's wife," said Väinämöinen.

"And you must be another drunk he dragged home from some bar," she said.

"I'm sorry I startled you, and, yes, your suspicions are correct. Heikki and I did meet in a bar. Let me introduce myself. My name is Väinämöinen, and I'm from Finland. I'm a famous musician over there."

Heikki's wife studied the pathetic, disheveled soul who slept in strangers' toolsheds. Yes, he looked like a musician, with his long and dirty hair, his flowered shirt, and his funny round hat. "What's that under your arm?"

"That's my instrument," said Väinämöinen. "My kantele. I'm the greatest player in the world, now or ever."

"And you're humble, too," Heikki's wife pointed out. "I'm going to dig up a few new potatoes for my breakfast. Since you're probably hungry and thirsty, you can join me for fried potatoes and coffee, and then you should probably leave."

Väinämöinen helped Heikki's wife with the potatoes by digging around in the dirt after she softened the soil with a manure fork. He collected a dozen tiny potatoes, some the size of golf balls, others slightly larger. They went inside. In the kitchen, Heikki's wife poured Väinämöinen a large cup of very strong coffee and then busied herself with cleaning and slicing the potatoes and dropping the slices into a melted pat of sizzling butter in a frying pan. As she chopped onion and added it to the potatoes, Väinämöinen played her a tune about the playful girls of Vaasa.

Soon they ate. Heikki still reeked and snored in the living room. Heikki's wife talked at first about trivial things—the weather and the garden—but then the conversation turned to her husband. She told Väinämöinen how disappointed she had become in him in recent years. "He drinks too much, brags too much and never accomplishes anything. I'd like to have the earlier Heikki back again," she said.

Väinämöinen decided that he owed this good woman a favor. After all, he shouldn't have gotten drunk with her husband, and he certainly should not have collapsed for the night in her toolshed. "In Finland, I'm a great man," he told Heikki's wife. "I'm the greatest of all musicians. I can perform great magical deeds with my music. You make wonderful coffee, and the potatoes were delicious. Therefore, I will perform a magical deed for you. I grant you one wish. Whatever you want me to do, I'll do it for you."

Heikki's wife sighed aloud at Väinämöinen's offer. *Here is another deluded drunk,* she thought. *Maybe he's crazy. He could even be a little dangerous.* She decided to appease him, to play along with his fantasy, if it made him happy. Plus, some of his mannerisms reminded her of her father. Her father had migrated to America from Karelia early in the century. She remembered how upset her father had been when the Soviet Union took Karelia and other eastern areas away from Finland at the end of World War II. The knowledge that his village had been ceded to the Russians had broken her father's heart, and he had died shortly afterwards.

"I want to show you something," Heikki's wife told Väinämöinen. "Wait here." She disappeared for a few minutes into the other end of the house. When she returned, she held an historical atlas of Finland, written in Finnish. She turned to the pages that showed the size of Finland at the beginning of the war and the size after the war. "If you want to do one thing for me, restore these stolen lands to Finland," she told Väinämöinen. "It will make me and my long-dead father very happy."

Väinämöinen felt very bad. "That's the kind of wish that can't be realized," he said. "I could sing into Siberia all of the Russians who now live there, but that would be unfair to them. Many are innocent of Stalin's long-ago actions. I could sing Finns into Karelia, but they already have settled lives somewhere else and would not want to be there. I can't redo the past."

"Well, that's it, then," said Heikki's wife. "I have work to do and will get no help from my husband. You probably have somewhere to go, too."

Heikki settled his pack on his shoulders and tucked his kantele under his arm. He headed for the front door, Heikki's wife following to see him out. As they passed Heikki, still passed out on the couch, the old man snorted loudly in his sleep and rolled over. A fresh wave of odor wafted up from him. Heikki's wife glared at her husband with distaste. "If you won't grant me my first wish," she told Väinämöinen, "then grant me this one: Make my husband into the man he used to be, the man he was thirty years ago."

Väinämöinen looked down at Heikki and realized the impossibility of this second request. Heikki was clearly beyond anyone's redemption. Heikki's hair was so dirty that it seemed to be coated thickly with axle grease. He stank of many layers of sweat, and his clothes smelled of rotting fish and other undefined decaying matter. He smelled of unwashed socks, insecticide, and stale beer. With each breath, Heikki whistled through his nostrils, snorted and gasped as if he were choking, but he slept on. Strange gurgling sounds issued from deep inside his body. His bowels rumbled ominously. Väinämöinen withdrew from his vicinity.

"The first task you gave me is clearly impossible," he told Heikki's wife. "But the second task is even more impossible than the impossible. Therefore, I think it's better that I take a closer look at those maps of yours," he said. "Maybe there's something I can do. Then I'll be on my way. And why is it, old woman, that you mere humans always expect to solve the impossible?"

"Because of love," said Heikki's wife.

As it turned out, love was a mystery that had baffled Väinämöinen for at least a thousand years. He didn't want to get into that. "Have somebody fax me copies of those maps," he told Heikki's wife and gave her his business card, with the fax number in the corner. Then he departed.

Misery Bay

Chapter Eight

Uuno

The men from Misery Bay who survived World War II returned home with their stories by the end of 1945, but Uuno went right on soldiering. After a while, he had been gone so long that he felt detached from the little hamlet where he had grown up. He felt he had lived through a long line of lives since leaving home. Early in the war, he and his outfit had landed on Guadalcanal, ostensibly to mop up, but in actuality they dug in and fought for months in sporadic hand-to-hand combat with a stubborn enemy. After that, Uuno and his fellow Marines participated in campaigns all over the Pacific—every one a little closer to Japan. Uuno was among those who landed in the Philippines a short time after McArthur's return. Later still, he fought on Peleliu and Angaur in Palau and finally fought on Saipan, where the Marines drove the Japanese into the hills and along the spine of the island until thousands committed suicide by leaping from the eight-hundred-foot cliffs at the end of the island.

By then, Uuno was one of only a handful of survivors of his original group. After the surrender, he and the others became occupiers in Japan. Finally, in late 1946, Uuno was given the opportunity to go home to an America that had stopped celebrating its victory and gotten on with post-war life. Instead of going home, Uuno reenlisted. He knew why. For a long time, he had been surrounded by death, destruction, and killing. He himself had looked into the face of the enemy and killed. The killing had emptied him out, had made him into a new kind of a man very different from the boy who had left Misery Bay in January of 1942 and joined the Marines. In Misery Bay, Uuno had been sure of himself and sure of his relationship to a forgiving Lutheran God. Uuno found himself no longer sure of himself, and he had lost God somewhere on Guadalcanal. He had felt utterly alone and abandoned on Peleliu and Angaur even as he and the other Marines fiercely supported each other. On Saipan, he had fought like a somnolent caught up in a nightmare but distanced from it even as it rushed through him. He felt punch drunk all the time.

He needed to heal, and Uuno saw the vast Pacific as a great healer. He had fallen in love with the beauty of the islands and of the islanders. He loved the way the Pacific Islanders blended into their environment and used the natural wealth of the islands and the lagoons. Nothing seemed wasted or despoiled. He saw a harmony in their lives that he lacked. He didn't want to return home a shell of a man. And, so, he stayed.

He had heard that on Saipan that navigators in the Caroline Islands still knew how to sail a canoe all over the Pacific without the aid of a map or a compass and sextant. The idea intrigued him. Before the war, Uuno had worked with his fisherman father on their small boat on Lake Superior. They had sold their catch of trout, whitefish, and herring to a local fishing co-operative. As a boy, Uuno had known the fear generated by fog on the big lake, and a number of times he had been terrified by fierce storms blowing out of Canada and creating immense waves that tossed their small craft from huge wave to huge wave. In winter, ice formed so thick on the deck and bows that the boat wallowed and threatened to sink. Still, with the aid of their instruments, the Coast Guard and lighthouses, they had always found their way back home.

For his month's leave, Uuno bummed a ride on a Navy seaplane and flew to an obscure spit of land in the Carolines called Satawal. On Satawal, Uuno met a navigator, an old man who was about to leave on a month-long trip to Saipan, a thousand miles away. The old man traveled simply, with a flagon of water, coconuts, and some dried fish and taro. He had no purpose for the long journey other than that his father and his father's father had done it. The old man wanted to refresh his own knowledge of the sea path so that he could, upon his return, pass that information down to his grandson.

In exchange for a knife, Uuno hitched a ride and, for the next thirty-two days, put his faith in the silent old man as they bobbed together across a vast stretch of the open Pacific. Twice they stopped at uninhabited islands to collect coconuts for fresh water and to fish the reefs. They smoked the fish in thick layers of leaves. For much of the trip, Uuno read *Moby Dick*, observed the navigator without discovering any of his secrets, and fished for tuna, whose dry pink meat was tasty even when raw.

The Pacific stretched out forever in every direction, an indifferent force both comforting and to be feared. Eventually, the old Satawalese and Uuno sighted Saipan on the horizon, and hours later they pulled the canoe up to the beach so that Uuno could rejoin civilization two days late. Uuno's skin was burned dark by the sun and dried by the salt, but his soul was full of the wonder of God. He no longer felt empty.

The years immediately following the war were the happiest of Uuno's life. He asked for and got a transfer to the tiny island of Rongelap in the Marshall chain. By then, he was a Marine sergeant. On Rongelap, he acted as a one-man security team for meteorologists subordinate to the atomic testing teams on nearby Bikini Atoll. Rongelap was one of the smallest, most isolated places on Earth and also one of the most beautiful. The Marshallese watched with curiosity as the meteorologists used high atmosphere balloons to judge air currents and sophisticated radio equipment to communicate with Bikini. Clearly, the Marshallese saw the visitors as entertainers, but they were no threat, so Uuno had little to do.

He abandoned the Navy cruiser anchored off the island and moved into a traditional Marshallese hut with a thatched roof, a raised wooden floor, hand-hewn corner posts, and woven mats for furnishings. The mats were uncomfortable, so Uuno brought a couple of mattresses from the ship and constructed a couple of rough chairs out of native woods. Uuno's stove consisted of a ring of stones in the yard. He added a grate and a pot from the ship and made a fire from wood collected in the nearby forest.

After the horror of war, Uuno loved the slow and harmonious rhythm of island life. It was like being a twelve-year-old Boy Scout on a camping trip once again but on a permanent basis. Uuno loved the strong sense of community among the Marshallese. The children swam together or played games together, while the adults repaired tools, canoes, and buildings together and gathered and prepared food together. Often multiple families ate together and then formed groups in the evening to sing or to gossip together. Uuno especially liked the Marshallese indifference to sins Uuno had been taught in Sunday School at the Lutheran Church in Misery Bay. Although adultery was extremely rare on the island, sex was not. Young, single girls slept with whoever was attractive to them. One of these young women appeared in Uuno's hut late one night and, thereafter, reappeared every night for several weeks. Her name was Justina. Her long, black hair streamed down her back to her waist. Her large, intelligent eyes were a fathomless brown, and her complexion—the color of creamed coffee—was wonderfully smooth and clean. Uuno used gestures to invite her to stay, and she moved in permanently, becoming his wife in Marshallese eyes and his mistress in the eyes of the meteorologists.

Uuno got along well with his in-laws. He couldn't speak Marshallese, and they couldn't speak English, so they communicated with each other by doing. Uuno helped them out with their tasks, and they, in turn, helped him with his. He and his Marshallese wife communicated beautifully at night in the privacy of their intimate moments.

Gradually, Uuno learned some Marshallese. He supplied his in-laws with Spam and corned beef, tools, flashlights, lamps, cloth, and other manufactured goods from the ship, and they taught him to fish with their kind of net, to find food in the forest and lagoon. He grew to love breadfruit with a coconut cream sauce and baked taro with smoked reef fish. He all but abandoned his uniform for a simple *thu*, and his body grew dark and firm.

He took frequent walks along the beach and often canoed across the lagoon to uninhabited islands too small to support permanent human habitation. Sometimes he spent all day alone, browsing among the tangled botanical garden that made up each uninhabited island. The smallest islands were used as pig pens by the Rongelapese, and sometimes Uuno would startle half-wild pigs that would race off through the underbrush, squealing loudly.

Less than a year after Uuno's arrival on Rongelap, his Marshallese wife presented him with a son. Uuno named the boy Martti after his grandfather, the Lake Superior fisherman far away in northern Michigan. The baby had the dark hair of a Pacific islander but the blue eyes of a Finn. The first time that Uuno held the baby, he spoke to him in Finnish. "The blood of fishermen flows through you from your mother's people and mine," he told the little one. "Some day you will grow up to be the greatest fisherman of them all."

In the first two years of Uuno's sojourn on the island, atomic tests were completed on Bikini without a hitch. Bikini and its lagoon were irradiated by the blasts, but the Bikinians had been moved safely away to another island. The deadly cloud of radiation was carried harmlessly away to the northeast by the wind currents.

Like everyone else on Rongelap, Uuno had a lot of free time. From the ship's library, Uuno took a series of books by a man named Vardis Fisher. Several of the books were about the desert ascetics of the early Church. The ascetics sought God in the emptiness of the desert. Uuno sought God in the emptiness of the Pacific. His Marshallese father-in-law taught him the rudiments of canoeing and of traditional navigation. With the further aid of a star guide from the ship, Uuno learned to read the stars. He would lie on his back at night in the bottom of the beached canoe and pick out individual stars and constellations. Later still, he would take the canoe out into the darkness of the lagoon and read the heavens to the rhythmic bobbing as waves and currents carried the canoe into unknown darkness. At such times, Uuno felt once more that he was a babe cradled away from the insanity of the larger world.

Eventually, Uuno gained enough Marshallese to be able to communicate with his Marshallese family and the other Rongelapese. Then his father-in-law took him in the outrigger beyond the sheltered lagoon into the open Pacific. Uuno learned to read the sun, currents, prevailing winds, swells and eddies, birds and fish. He learned to hoist and lower a sail smoothly and rapidly. He learned to compensate for the drag of the outrigger. Eventually he sailed alone into the open ocean where he drifted for hours, fishing. He sought God in the vastness of the sky and the measureless horizon. Once he caught a shark longer than the canoe. After hours of labor, he brought it aside the canoe and shot it twice in the head. The creature's death throes nearly capsized him. He tied the shark along the canoe's length and sailed with great difficulty back to Rongelap where the whole village ate shark steaks, and the men drank kava late into the night.

On Bikini, the Navy and the scientists were ready to perform another atomic test. On Rongelap, the meteorologists tested the winds, which were blowing directly from Bikini to Rongelap. They informed the authorities on Bikini and assumed the test would be delayed until the winds shifted. But, this time, the test went off right on schedule anyway. By radio, the meteorologists and their crews were told to don protective gear and to cruise out to sea in a southwesterly direction until they were clear of the radioactive drift. "They knew damned well the cloud would be carried right over Rongelap," the chief meteorologist told Uuno as he and the others donned their hot and clumsily heavy anti-contamination suits. "Just beyond here are the atolls of Rongerik, Utirik, Taka, and Bikar. They're all populated. What in the hell do they think they're doing?"

Uuno wanted to know if the cruiser could take his wife and child aboard. The chief meteorologist asked the high command on Bikini. Permission was flatly refused. Uuno argued with the meteorologists but to no avail. "We have to get out of here now," he was told by the cruiser's captain. "We can't leave you behind. If you try to stay, we'll drag you aboard at gunpoint. Orders are orders!"

Uuno and the other Americans boarded the light cruiser and left Rongelap as quickly as possible, the engines on full, and the deck vibrating with a low hum. A few hours later, the sea seethed and hissed and took on an oily appearance. The surface gave off iridescent colors like the skin of a snake. Back on Rongelap, huge waves slammed into the island, nearly inundating it. Then a gray snow began to fall until the island was coated several inches deep in the strange, light stuff. The Marshallese had never seen snow before. The children played in it and ate it. The adults were baffled by it.

In ensuing weeks, again and again Uuno tried to get back to Rongelap, but he was told that the entire northern Marshalls were out of bounds to him and to anyone else without a permit from the Navy and the Atomic Energy Commission. The Rongelapese had been guaranteed a new home on a distant but unnamed island.

A few months after the so-called accident, Uuno learned through medical officers that his son had died of leukemia. His wife had many mystifying health problems related to radioactivity. She and the other survivors were under constant medical study by teams of Navy doctors. In certain circles, the Rongelapese were quite famous. They were even flown to a government hospital outside Washington, D.C., where they were put into a kind of lab and monitored twenty-four hours a day for several weeks. Then they were flown back to the Pacific and requarantined somewhere on a Navy base in Micronesia. Uuno tried to see Justina but was rebuffed. "You have no marriage certificate and no right to see her," he was told. Her whereabouts remained a mystery.

Uuno grew increasingly bitter. Although no one would talk about it, he knew that the Marshallese had been intentionally irradiated so that they could be studied. They were part of an experiment called Operation Bravo. The military couldn't use Americans as guinea pigs, so they had chosen the Marshallese because they had no political voice and were naïve and pliable and isolated.

After he was notified of the death of his wife, Uuno left the Marines and returned to Misery Bay and the world of his boyhood. Uuno's friends and family in Misery Bay had already heard hundreds of war stories by then and were not interested in Uuno's version of the war. America was in the midst of a post-war boom, and nobody was interested in hearing any negative stories about the government either. When Uuno tried to explain to another veteran of the Pacific Theatre what had happened to his Marshallese family, Uuno got no sympathy. "Them islanders live like animals," the veteran replied. "They ain't no better than niggers."

135

Uuno needed to escape from people like that, so he rejoined his dad on the fishing boat. Uuno and his dad spent long days isolated on the great lake, and at night they repaired equipment and worked on the boat. Still, Uuno felt a great emptiness inside and needed to fill the void by telling somebody what had happened to him. He began to spend nearly every evening at the Mosquito Inn, where he would trap somebody into listening to him. He would tell the listener that the earlier Uuno was dead. "If the war hadn't come, I'd've become a successful fisherman or logger. I'd've married a Copper Country girl, and I'd already have several kids and a four-bedroom house," he'd say. "Instead I can find no meaning in any of that. The men I fought alongside are mostly dead. They'll never again eat a steak or cheer the Tigers or make love."

A lot of the listeners were returned veterans with their own war stories. Most had already taken jobs, married, joined a church and gotten on with life. They were affronted by Uuno's inability to do the same. "Put it behind you," they'd say. "Forget the Marshallese girl. She was just part of the past—part of your war experience. Form a real relationship with a pretty Finnish girl. Start dating."

Uuno hated the whole idea of dating—of playing the elaborate games that were necessary to catch a wife. He wouldn't listen to the girls' incessant gossip, and he cared nothing about their cliques and feuds. He refused to be fashionable and didn't keep up with popular music and dance crazes and movies. Mostly he worked hard with his dad on the boat and then drank at the end of the bar in the Mosquito.

Eventually, because no one would listen, Uuno began to tell elaborate lies about his experiences. The lies disgusted him. When the patrons of the Mosquito Inn began to avoid him, Uuno began to hang around a particularly scuzzy bar in nearby South Range. For a while, Uuno liked going there because none of the patrons sought any meaning to life beyond the effects of the next bottle of Old Milwaukee. Plus, none of them had any pretensions to being part of the local *in*-crowd. One of the regulars was Toby Santti, who had recently moved to South Range from the tiny hamlet of Watton. Toby took fierce pride in being able to yowl like a wolf in heat. When Toby was very drunk, he was especially good at yowling at the moon. Sometimes he would go outside to yowl, but most of the time, he would sit at the bar and yowl strenuously, the cords in his neck bulging from tension as the high-pitched, rising sound burst from his throat. Afterwards, people all up and down the bar bought Toby drinks, and he was happy. "I can bleat like a sheep, too," he told them.

"Ya, and I can fart like a horse!" roared some wit at the end of the bar, and everybody except Uuno laughed uproariously. One young drunk laughed so hard that he began to choke on his Old Milwaukee. When the young man couldn't seem to get his breath and collapsed to the floor, turning blue, everyone laughed over that, too. When the young man vomited at the base of a bar stool, other patrons told him he was gross. They stopped laughing and focused on some more serious drinking and light conversation, interspersed with more jokes about the guy still lying on the floor in his puddle of vomit.

After a while, the young man rose from the floor and staggered off to the toilet. He didn't return. Toby let out another ear-shattering yelp and received some more free drinks. *Is this what wartime friends died for?* Uuno wondered as he surveyed the crowd. *Did my Marshallese family suffer as guinea pigs so that Toby can be free to yowl like a wolf?*

The next day, Uuno had a hangover but fished all day on Superior with his dad. Late in the afternoon, they snagged the nets and ripped huge, ragged holes in one of them. After they docked and unloaded their catch, they debated whether or not to repair the nets themselves but decided against it. Uuno brought the nets to a man in Betsey who repaired them for a living. When Uuno returned home, it was late, and Uuno's dad announced that they were taking a few days off. "But it's the height of the commercial fishing season," argued Uuno.

"Some things are more important than catching fish," replied Uuno's father. "You are my son, and you have a sickness in your soul and a bitterness in your heart. I thought that time would cure your wounds, but it hasn't. Ever since we got indoor plumbing a few years ago, we've stopped using the sauna. I haven't done repairs, and now it's in pretty rough shape. We're going to build the family a new one, starting tomorrow. A sauna is a holy place for Finns. In the old days, our children were born there. When we were sick, we went there for a cure. The dead were once laid out in the sauna and prepared for God."

Early the following morning, Uuno and his dad gathered picks and shovels, axes and saws, and a box of tools and walked behind the house to a stand of birches. They roughly marked out the foundation of the sauna in the earth and cleared the area. Then Uuno's dad pointed to a swathe of grass and moss nearby that was a deeper green than the surrounding greenery. "That rich color is either from a buried spring or from an ancient streambed," he said.

They took turns softening the earth with picks and shoveling out the dirt. About three feet down, they hit a broad layer of rocks and pebbling. "There's the streambed," said Uuno's dad. "Long before white men claimed this land, this must have been a small river." They finished rounding off the spring hole, and then lined it with an old rain slicker and with Marine Corps canvas tenting that Uuno had brought back from the Pacific. They covered the lining with good-sized rocks, all the way up to ground level. "The lining will prevent it from silting up and getting muddy," said Uuno's dad.

In the following days, Uuno and his dad cut cedar logs from a formerly useless swampy corner of their property. The logs gave off a rich, aromatic smell as the men peeled them. Afterwards, their gloves, sleeves, and arms were streaked black with sticky sap, and their shirts and pants were stiff and thick with the stuff. They tightly grooved each log as they built the sauna. They used clay for the chinking. They lined the inside of the sauna with boards from a lumberyard in Houghton. The floor was pine. The roof was finished off in the old way with wooden shingles. Finally, Uuno's dad put in a wood-fired sauna stove with a drop box and grate for ashes. The rocks were picked by hand from the beach at Misery Bay. Each stone was round and smooth from eons of wave action and each contained rich bands of color—browns, yellow, greens, whites, grays, dark reds.

Finally, the sauna was ready to be initiated. Uuno and his dad heated the rocks for hours on a Saturday evening. They cut fresh cedar boughs

138

to sting each other's flesh into cleanliness. They undressed in a tiny ante-room and then went inside and sat on the new cedar benches. Uuno reached into a bucket of cold spring water with a ladle and splashed a little onto the rocks. Steam hissed, a rock popped, and a wave of heat struck Uuno's shoulders and ears. Uuno's dad dipped the cedar boughs into the bucket of water and sprinkled the water from the boughs onto the rocks. The room took on the rich smell of the forest. Uuno breathed slowly but deeply. He felt pleasantly on fire.

After a while, he and his dad went outside and poured buckets of very cold spring water over each other. Then they went back inside.

They repeated this ritual three times. By then Uuno felt cleansed in body and spirit. He felt close to his father, to the people of his hamlet, to nature, and to God. It was the first time he had felt that way since Operation Bravo.

Uuno's healing was not yet complete. In ensuing months, he periodically became depressed. Uuno had never had any interest in sport fishing, maybe because he made his living fishing commercially on Lake Superior. But in January a Marine Corps veteran friend asked Uuno to go fishing for sturgeon through the ice. When Uuno balked at the idea, the friend told Uuno that sturgeon fishing was different. "It's a kind of communion with nature," the friend said.

Uuno said he didn't understand.

"You'll see what I mean when we get there," said the ex-Marine, who carried a lot of German metal in his legs and who found walking difficult.

At the lake, Uuno pulled the ice shanty over the frozen surface while his crippled friend struggled to keep up. The shanty was on runners and moved easily over the smooth ice. They broke a large hole in the ice with a crow bar. Uuno chipped the edges until the hole was uniformly round. His friend scooped out the ice chips with a spade and sent them sailing down the ice. Then they slid the shanty over the hole and were ready for fishing. They stood a heavily weighted pronged spear on the edge of the hole. A thick line was attached to the spear. Coils of line lay looped beside the spear, and the end of the line was tied to a sturdy nail protruding from a wall of the shanty. A small chair folded out from the shanty wall and Uuno sat on it and stared into the hole in the ice.

"Now what do I do?" asked Uuno.

"Nothing," said the friend. "Sturgeon fishing is like joining a monastery. You have to remain very still and totally quiet. Otherwise you'll scare the fish."

The ex-Marine dumped a foul-smelling bucket of bait into the hole. It settled twenty feet down on the bottom. "All you have to do is stare at the lake bottom and wait for a sturgeon to swim by. Then you drop the spear."

"And what chance do we have that a sturgeon will conveniently swim into view?" asked Uuno.

"Slim to none," said the ex-Marine. "But nearly every winter somebody manages to spear one. It just takes days and days of persistence. Maybe this year it'll be us."

"And what are the attributes of a good sturgeon fisherman?" asked Uuno.

"Patience, my friend, patience," said the ex-Marine. "You just have to stare into that hole day and night until a sturgeon appears. Sturgeon are bottom feeders, and they're huge. One of 'em will gobble up the bait in a couple of seconds. Those seconds may be your only chance to spear one. That's why you can't relax. Just keep your eyes focused on the bottom. The season only lasts a couple of weeks."

"This is crazy," said Uuno.

"It's good for your soul," said the ex-Marine. "But my soul is okay, so I'm going to cut smaller holes outside and fish for perch. Plus, I'll be your go-fer. I'll cook us some warm food—beans and hotdogs mostly—over the Sterno, and I'll sleep in the truck. I'm not man enough to stare into that hole. I'll leave that to you."

The ex-Marine left, and Uuno could hear him punching holes in the ice with the crow bar. Then he could hear him placing lines and setting flags. The crippled veteran had brought his dog with him. The dog ran around on the lake ice for a couple of hours, but then scratched at the shanty door, and

Uuno let him in. The dog was a mongrel, half grown and full of energy. Uuno liked having the little fellow around.

Uuno stared into the hole. At the surface, the water was green and streaked with light. Near the bottom, the green was thicker and darker but amazingly clear. Uuno could see every pebble on the muddy bottom and thought he could make out individual grains of sand. The bait stood out brightly against the green water and brown bottom.

For three days, Uuno stared through the hole in the ice. At night, he hung a kerosene lamp directly above the hole, and the thin light filtered down to the bottom, creating a circle of light in impenetrable darkness. By the third day, Uuno felt he was alone in the world, except for the dog, and that he was staring into the eye of God. He felt at peace. He waited.

In the late afternoon of the fifth day, just as the gray winter light was fading on the horizon and the light at the bottom of the lake was reduced to a trickle, a dark shadow loomed on the edge of the hole. Uuno had been cata-tonic for hours, so it took him a second to react. By then a huge sturgeon had filled the lake bottom directly below the hole. Instinctively, Uuno's arm reached out, grasped the weighted spear and dropped it straight into the hole. The heavy spear dropped in a silent rush straight toward the bottom, its prongs burying themselves, in less than a second, into the broad back of the sturgeon.

A moment later, much of the coiled line had disappeared through the hole, and the sturgeon was gone. Uuno grabbed the fast-disappearing line, looped part of the rope around his back and part of it over the nail, and held on. When the line went taut, Uuno nearly fell headfirst into the hole.

For the next several hours, Uuno and the sturgeon were locked in combat, then Uuno slowly began to gain ground. He brought in coil after coil of line, but his arms were cramping, and his head ached from the exertion. The dog sensed something momentous and peered anxiously into the hole, his tail wagging furiously. Finally, the giant fish came into view and, as Uuno pulled with all his waning strength, the monster rose toward the surface. When it was close enough, Uuno reached down into the icy water and grabbed the end of the spear. Then he brought the sturgeon quickly to the surface by straddling the hole and pulling the spear out hand over hand.

As the fish emerged, Uuno saw that it was yards long. He had never imagined anything so big. *It's the Moby Dick of Lake Superior*, Uuno thought as the fish reached the surface. "I've caught one of God's greatest creations," Uuno said aloud but to himself. As he hoisted the creature out of the hole, the exertion caused Uuno to fall over backwards. He struck his head on the ice.

The monster fish terrified the little dog. He rushed in a circle around the tight confines of the shanty and then leaped into the hole the fish had just vacated. In an instant, the dog was gone—swept under the ice. Seconds later, the sturgeon demolished the shanty, its huge tail smashing walls into kindling and sending the pieces flying in all directions. Uuno tried to get to his feet, but the tail struck him at the knees and sent him skidding across the ice. He had enough presence of mind to hold onto the line tightly. When he finally got to his feet, he pulled the sturgeon away from the hole. Already it was suffocating in the crisp winter air.

A hundred feet away, the crippled ex-Marine still stood over one of his tiny fishing holes. Then he let out an odd yelp and reached down into the hole. A moment later, he pulled out his wild-eyed dog. "Where in the hell did you come from?" he said in disbelief. Then he watched as the shanty all but exploded with the pounding fish.

The poor dog shook uncontrollably from hypothermia. The ex-Marine slipped off his jacket and wrapped the freezing dog in its warmth.

A few minutes later, the sturgeon lay dead. "My God, it's longer than my truck," said Uuno.

"You and your damned fish destroyed my ice shanty and nearly killed my dog," said the ex-Marine.

Other ice fishermen had heard or seen the commotion and came to investigate. Once they saw what lay in the splinters of the ice shanty, they approached with awe. One man took off his hat and stood in silence as if he were in the presence of God.

Uuno became famous as the man who had caught the giant fish. At the Mosquito Inn, other men stood him drinks. "That fish was the soul of Lake Superior," a drunk told Uuno.

Uuno accepted his fame quietly and had the sturgeon stuffed. Over his mother's objections, he tried to hang it across the living room above the couch, but its weight caused the wall to sag. Eventually, Uuno had to accept the fact that a fish of that size and weight would not fit anywhere. He and his dad dragged it outside and, with great difficulty, hoisted it on top of the wood stacked the length of the garage along the back wall. The stack collapsed under its weight. Uuno left it there while he built a long and narrow kind of mausoleum with a picture window. Behind the window, in the back yard, Uuno interred the fish.

The sturgeon became a tourist attraction. The Houghton County Chamber of Commerce advertized it in a brochure. A book about ridiculous roadside attractions included it, along with a gigantic dinosaur in California and a fifty-foot cow in North Dakota. Uuno charged a dollar to see it. He began to feel better about himself and the world in general. He occasionally went to church and felt God's presence in the rainbow of light streaming through the stained glass. At church, he met a half-French, half-Finnish, green-eyed and brown-haired beauty. Six months later they got married.

Uuno never went ice fishing for sturgeon again. "Staring once into the eye of God is enough," he said.

When he and his wife had a son, they named the boy Martti after the grandfather. The wife never knew why Uuno insisted that the boy's middle name be Marshall. When she asked about it, Uuno said the name reminded him of another little boy, one who had never had a chance to go fishing with his dad. "It'll be different with our son," he told his wife.